A SWEET FAMILIARITY

Also by Daoma Winston

DAOMA WINSTON

A SWEET FAMILIARITY

Futura
Macdonald & Co
London & Sydney

A Futura Book

First published in Great Britain in 1983
by Macdonald & Co (Publishers) Ltd
London & Sydney

This Futura edition published in 1984

Copyright © Daoma Winston 1981

ISBN 0 7088 2475 7

Reproduced, printed and bound in Great Britain by
Hazell Watson & Viney Limited,
Member of the BPCC Group,
Aylesbury, Bucks

Futura Publications
A Division of
Macdonald & Co (Publishers) Ltd
Maxwell House
74 Worship Street
London EC2A 2EN

A BPCC plc Company

For JOHN FRANKLIN, artist, and BOB HOPPER, sculptor, who saw the story begin

A SWEET
FAMILIARITY

PROLOGUE

There had always been Vickerys and Paiges in the town of Meadowville. The first of them were with the pioneer families that settled a hundred and seventy-seven miles northwest of St. Louis at a trail crossing used by hunting mountain men and foraging Indians.

By the late 1840s, when the village had spread through the small bowl-shaped valley beneath a cliff called Dead Man's Bluff, a Paige Saloon had been built across from the Vickery Bank on Main Street and a Paige Park had been laid out facing the Vickery Mercantile. There was a Vickery Street, a Paige Boulevard, and some talk of a Vickery-Paige Inn, which came to nothing.

The fortunes of both families rose and fell with those of the town, but they did better than most. By 1970, the town's population had fallen to forty-six thousand and there no longer existed a Paige Saloon or a Vickery Mercantile, yet Morgan Paige was still a judge on the state circuit court and Dane Vickery was president of the family bank called the First

Meadowville Farmers and Mechanics Bank.

Both were important men in the town and had been good friends all their lives. It was of this that Dane Vickery thought as he watched Vernon Meese, the last member of the board of directors to arrive, finally take his seat at the long oak table.

"Sorry I'm late," Vernon said, smoothing the bushy wings of blond hair on either side of his small head. "The aldermen's meeting ran overtime as usual."

He didn't have to explain that as the newest and youngest member of the council he didn't feel free to slip away before the gavel banged recess. The other men present understood.

Dane nodded acknowledgment, still thinking of his friendship with Morgan Paige, and settled into his chair. He was a big man, broad in the shoulder and chest, though not tall. His dark-brown hair was thick and his mustache was full. Bright-eyed, ruddy cheeked, virile, he looked far younger than his fifty-two years . . . Today, however, he felt much older. For the second time in his life something had died in him. He put no name to it, knowing only that its going had thinned his sap to water and had made ashes of his soul . . .

Slowly he raised his blue eyes to look in the face of each of the seven men present, as if he were directing his words to each of them individually rather than as a group. It was at Morgan Paige that he looked last and longest.

Finally he spoke, his voice rasping but quiet. "You all know why we're here."

The men were silent for a moment. Then Morgan Paige cleared his throat. "What about minutes?" he asked. "Shouldn't somebody make a record?"

Morgan Paige's suggestion was reflective not only of his judicial experience but also of his judicious temperament. He

10

was a man who liked chess and intimate conversation and slow silent walks in snowy fields. He was slender to the point of frailty, white haired, with a narrow wrinkled face and thin lips. Although he was only five years older than Dane, he seemed out of an earlier generation—but that had never been a barrier to their friendship.

"I'll do the minutes," Vernon Meese offered eagerly. He reached for paper, pen. "Board of directors' minutes. August . . . now let's see . . ."

"The seventeenth," Dane told him.

"August 17," Vernon repeated, "in the year of 1970."

Dane waited until Vernon stopped writing and looked up expectantly. "We don't need to have an audit done."

"What's that?" Vernon asked.

Morgan Paige cleared his throat again. There were uncertain mumbles from the other men. The board of directors had voted at its last formal meeting to call in outside auditors.

"We don't need to have it done, I said. *I* took the money. And I'd prefer that you ask no questions. None are necessary."

"Dane!" Morgan Paige whispered into dead silence.

Dane didn't turn his head to look at his best friend. Slowly, softly, he repeated, "I took the money. And now I've brought it back."

Someone swore. Morgan Paige's mouth opened on a mute groan.

"It's here," Dane said. "In this bag under the table. Two hundred and fifty thousand dollars."

He got to his feet, went to the door. As he opened it, he said without looking back, "I prefer to be left alone. Thank you." Then he closed the door firmly, leaving chaos behind him.

His Cadillac was in the "no parking" zone in front of the

bank. Dane remembered when the bank had been called by the family name. It became the First Meadowville Farmers and Mechanics Bank in 1933, while his father cursed Franklin Roosevelt. Dane himself considered that it had been a good thing, in spite of the curses.

He made a u-turn in the center of Main Street, passing in front of the Sears Building, which stood on the spot once occupied by the Paige Saloon. He slowed at Paige Park, noting the rainbows that hung over the fountains built in memory of the town's sons, dead in three wars, both Vickerys and Paiges among them. Meadowville's state agriculture building stood on what had been the site of the Vickery Mercantile across the way.

He turned onto quiet, sun-filled Vickery Street and parked in the asphalt driveway beside the house. The house had been built in the 1890s, replacing one that had grown too small and that was perhaps too simple for the family's needs. It was a freshly painted white with green shutters, broad verandahs and the gingerbread decoration popular in its time. It had a scrubbed, well-manicured look, though there were no geraniums or African violets on the windowsills, no roses climbing the trellis against the side. Dane Vickery's house lacked the woman's touch, as did the man himself.

He had missed it for nineteen years, ever since his younger son, Claude, had murdered his wife Clara in childbirth. Dane knew he was wrong, unfair. But that was how he thought of it. Clara's death had been murder. And it was Claude who had done it, fighting, kicking, tearing his way out of her vulnerable body and into a world that didn't want or need him.

Dane mopped his brow with a crisp handkerchief before he

12

went inside. The house was quiet, cool, empty. He had expected no one to be there, knowing full well that his son John was still at the bank. John was a good son, he thought. Too bad that he hadn't yet married. A man of thirty-four shouldn't be alone. A man of fifty-two shouldn't be alone either . . . That was why it had happened. Because Clara had been killed, taken from him . . . Claude would be working at the service station, though Dane hadn't expected him to last out the whole summer there. The boy was nineteen, but it seemed he would never grow up. He was a dreamer, a stammerer. He wasn't much now, and never would be much. Dane knew that a man was supposed to love his sons equally, but he'd learned that they weren't always equally lovable.

He shrugged away the thought of Claude as he settled his bulk in the swivel chair behind his desk. The library was shadowed. Outside a mockingbird sang in the eaves. He listened until it went silent. Then he looked down at the desk top. It was cleared and neat. He had taken care of everything the night before. After seeing Ellen for the last time. Beautiful Ellen Paige. There was nothing else to do now . . .

It had all happened because he'd lost Clara. But what did it matter? he wondered. The single joyful year he had planned to prolong into forever was over. He knew that Ellen's decision was final, and that she would never change her mind. She had never felt for him what he'd felt for her. And he couldn't go on as before, betraying his best friend, the lover of his best friend's wife. With Ellen gone he didn't need the money. But now he was dishonored, an embezzler and thief to no purpose . . .

He took a pistol from the desk drawer, checked to see that

13

it was loaded. Then, with a single swift motion he held the gun to his temple and pulled the trigger.

His last thought was that he was putting an end to it. But ten years later the sound of the shot still echoed in Meadowville.

CHAPTER 1

On a bright mid-afternoon in mid-September of 1980, when a hush lay over street and lawn and house, Liz Paige leaned against her front door and listened, trembling, as the quiet whispers began.

Outside the old oaks in the front yard had already started to drop their leaves, so the long expanse of unkempt weed and brush appeared littered with mounds of gold and the sun warmed the low brick rambler built after the Second World War by Morgan Paige to replace a clapboard farmhouse put up seventy years before.

Inside, where Liz stood, it seemed cool and as if it were close to twilight. She had intended to go to the mailbox at the end of the drive, but now the envelopes she held fell unnoticed from her suddenly numbed fingers. For the whispering went on and on . . .

It wasn't a few words mumbled in restless sleep. It wasn't a sudden thought, spoken aloud in momentary absentmindedness. It was deliberate. Intense. It had been practiced silently for a long time before it was turned into sound. It was a prayer, an incantation, an invocation. And it was born of a wish beyond reality, the rotten fruit of a singular madness . . .

Liz understood. She had had time to learn. It began when she was fifteen, and now she was twenty-five.

She was tall, slender, with dark chestnut hair cut very short and hot blue eyes set wide apart under thick dark brows. She wore gray twill riding trousers and a sleeveless white shirt with a frayed collar.

Wincing, with the burn of held-back tears in her eyes and a chill in her flesh, she hurried across the hall and into a dim room, crying ahead, "Mom? Mom, are you all right?"

Ellen Paige half-lay, half-sat in her padded wheelchair, staring through limp lace curtains at the empty street. Her hair, once luxuriant auburn, was now white and wispy, drawn into a thin bun at the back of her neck. Her lips were colorless, and her once patrician features sagged. But there still remained the traces of a former charm. Her eyes were lavender and deep set under arching brows. Her mouth was sensual and soft. Her hands were fine, very pale and long fingered, expressive even at rest.

Now they were clenched into tight fists. She beat them on the arms of the chair and went on whispering, as if Liz hadn't spoken. Whispering in strained words that fell like small cold stones from her soft mouth. "Maggie, you must come home to me. Maggie . . . You must. Can you hear me, my Maggie? Come home. Come home."

"Mom?" Though she wanted to scream, Liz managed to speak quietly. "Mom, listen. It's me. It's Liz. I'm here. I'm with you. It's Liz."

Ellen Paige turned her head in slow motion. Her clenched

16

fists fell to her lap. "I know you're Liz," she said matter-of-factly. "I was talking to Maggie."

"Oh, please . . . please don't."

"I have to try, Liz. I *have* to. I'm not being willful. I don't want to upset you. I just have to try. Don't you understand? I know my love will bring her back. I know it, Liz. If only I have the strength to keep on trying."

"Maggie's dead," Liz said gently.

"I know that." There was stubborn patience in her voice, and certainty in her eyes.

"You saw her buried, mom. We stood together with dad. Don't you remember?"

Liz knew that reason was useless and that the argument was without point. Ellen couldn't understand. But Liz couldn't help herself. It was either that or scream. Or weep . . . A memory flickered in her. Her father's wrinkled face, sad eyes. She heard herself again, crying, *I can't stand it, dad!* And he answered, *What can I do? Do you want to go away?* And she said fiercely, *No, no! I can't do that.* And he asked, *Then shall I send your mother away?* And Liz screamed, *No, you can't do that either. . . .*

"I remember the day we buried Maggie," Ellen was saying. "She didn't deserve to die. She was at the beginning of her life. Not at the end of it. She was innocent, without blame. And she had the right to grow up and grow old."

"It was an accident, mom."

"I know. But it can't have really been the end. Her soul goes on. Why else would she have been born? Why would any of us have been born? Life can't end with death. It's wasteful. It wouldn't make sense. The soul can't die. It lives on."

"In its own way," Liz said. "Its own way, mom."

17

Ellen Paige went on as if she hadn't heard. "And since it does, then there's always the chance."

"No."

"If she hears me, if she wants to, I know she can come back."

Liz thought of her older sister Maggie, who had always said she could do anything. And it had seemed true then to Liz. Maggie . . . slipping past the room where their father played chess and tiptoeing into the night . . . returning hours later, unchallenged, to giggle, *I told you so,* in the dark. Maggie had always said she could do anything, and always believed it. And somehow it had seemed right, Because Maggie was Maggie.

"I can't give up. I can't forget. I have to try," Ellen murmured, the words ending on a gasp.

"I'll get you a pill," Liz said. She fumbled over the end table. Which one? Where was it? Why had the whispering suddenly begun again? The pill. The water. She leaned over her mother.

The older woman sat still, her head drooping against the back of the chair, her breath coming in small quick bursts. She opened tear-filled eyes, accepted the medication, swallowed it with a sip of water. With a murmured "thanks," she closed her eyes. "I must have her back, Liz. It's all that I live for. It has to be the way it used to be."

There had been a time when Liz would have pleaded, *But mom, you still have me. I'm here. I'm with you. What about me?* . . . But she knew better now. It wasn't that her mother didn't want her, Liz, but that her mother wanted Maggie, too. The both of them. The way it had been before.

"Rest," Liz said softly. "Rest, and let the pill work."

"I'm not crazy," her mother answered. "I know you think I am. You. Dr. Detrick. Everyone else. That's how people deal with things that they don't understand. Things that they're

18

afraid of. They say, 'Well, that's crazy!' And turn their eyes away. But I absolutely know what I know and feel. And sometimes, oh, Liz, sometimes I can feel her so close to me. I can feel her reaching out and trying to get through. Trying to come home to me. Where she belongs."

"Could you nap?" Liz asked hopefully. "It would do you good."

Her mother nodded. Liz was at the door when her mother said, "All right. I won't talk about it. Not if it bothers you. I'm not trying to bother you. But I want her back, Liz."

"Nap," Liz said softly. Trembling, she leaned against the wall. Circumstances had kept her busy, forced her to be practical. She wasn't given to imaginative speculations. She tried very hard to live in the present, not to dwell too much on the past. But now she remembered the woman her mother had been . . . Tall. Slim, but curved. Dark auburn hair piled high. A laughing woman. Slightly vain of her narrow waist and fine hands. Always dressed for company, for a party. Her smiles projecting a steady warmth . . . That woman was gone. Just as Maggie was gone. And with her, the giggles in the dark, the gleeful spinning of adventures, half-told, half-hinted at. Had they been true? Had they been false? Liz never knew for sure.

She told herself she should call Dr. Detrick. But it was so useless. He'd say, *There's nothing we can do.* He'd say, *We must be grateful that it isn't worse.* Liz *was* grateful. He'd say, *The real worry is that this obsession might create enough agitation to affect her heart. She can't afford that. You understand, my dear.* And the aneurysm on the aorta *was* the real danger. It had developed silently, slowly, over the years. Compared to that, the whispering was nothing.

19

But it terrified Liz nevertheless. If she listened too long, answered too sensibly, thought too hard on its words, she found herself wondering . . . What if . . . ? Suppose Maggie could . . . ? And Liz would remember that Maggie had always said she could do anything, anything she wanted to. With pounding heart and aching head, Liz would begin to wonder. Nobody in the world knew everything. There was no proof either way. What if . . . ? And then, immediately, she would ask herself what was happening to her.

She drew a deep shaky breath and went to the phone. Dr. Detrick said exactly what she had thought he would. And then: "It's come later than usual, hasn't it?"

"Yes. A month and a few days." She answered his question without comment. It had been useless to discuss it before. It would be useless now. She was certain that these were not yearly seizures that came with the dread anniversary and disappeared when it was safely past. She believed her mother thought of Maggie's return most of the time, but silently, and only expressed it aloud when the pressure became too great to hold it within.

"Interesting that it's later," the doctor observed.

"I thought it might be passing over."

"I'm not sure it would be good for that to happen, Liz. It would mean she'd given up hope."

"Yes," Liz agreed dully.

"Just watch her. And try not to worry."

"Yes," she repeated. She told him good-bye, put down the phone. The whispering had stopped now. With a glance at her watch and a sudden lightening of her heart she hurried down the hall. Richard would be coming soon.

They were sitting on the sofa. She was in one corner, he in the other. They looked like a young married couple relaxing with their drinks before dinner. But they weren't married, and he was beginning to wonder if they ever would be.

"And that's the way it is," Walter Cronkite said sadly from the television screen, "Friday, September 19. The 321st day of captivity for the American hostages in Iran."

Before the usual "good-night" sign-off, Liz pushed the remote-control button. The screen went dark. Silence fell. Sighing, she looked toward the dim hallway beyond the door.

"It's awful for them, Richard."

He understood her empathy for the distant strangers held under terrorist guns, and shifted close to her, settling his arm around her shoulders. "They've got a chance."

Richard Braun was twenty-seven years old and still an optimist, even though his work as a general practice small-town attorney exposed him daily to such a wide range of human frailties as might shatter any man's illusions. Yet he was unaffected, expecting the best but taking what came, which was often the worst.

Because he was an optimist, he went on. "And speaking of chances . . . Let's not wait any more, Liz. Let's get married."

She pressed closer to him. He could feel the warmth of her body in his. Her blue eyes were fixed on his face. "We can't. It's too much for you to take on. All this . . ." Her hands moved in a vague gesture. "Me. Mom. The way things are."

He caught her hands, drew them to his lips, and spoke into them. "I'm willing, Liz."

He knew she'd had a bad day. But she hadn't told him about it until he picked up the envelopes in front of the door.

When she saw him holding them and caught his quizzical look, she had said, "I was going to put them out for the mailman . . ." In a shaky voice she had told him the rest of it.

Now he touched the frown between her brows, smoothed back a soft chestnut curl. "All right. But I want you to think about it some more. And don't take too long. I want a wife. Which means you. I want a home. And that means wherever I can get it. My place. Here. It's okay with me."

Whispering, her eyes suddenly bright with tears, she said, "Oh, Richard, I want to, want to so much. But the way things are . . ."

And how could they change? he asked himself. Her mother's aneurysm wouldn't go away. She wouldn't learn to walk again. And was there a miracle to heal the wounds of the past?

He said only, "We could make it work."

"Maybe," but her voice was doubtful. She slid from under his arm and got up. "Want to stay for potluck dinner?" At his nod, she went on. "I'll see if mom will join us."

She was at the door when the phone rang. He made as if to rise, but she waved him back and answered it, saying, after a moment, "It's for you, Richard."

It was the girl from the answering service. "Mr. Braun, Dr. Detrick just called. He said to tell you that John Vickery has died."

Richard thanked her and put down the phone. He had known for a year that it was coming. Now that it had happened he felt only dread. He'd have to tell Liz about John . . . And about his younger brother Claude.

Liz was watching Richard, a question in her eyes.

"I guess I can't stay after all, Liz." he said.

"Is something wrong?"

"Check on your mother and come back. I want to talk to you before I go."

She gave him a puzzled look, then hurried away.

The light seemed to follow her from the room. He had experienced the same thing many times since he'd fallen in love with her. But he'd never gotten used to it. And he never would.

After a few moments, she returned. "What is it?"

"Your mother all right?"

"She's slept. She seems better."

"Then don't look so worried. It'll be okay. You've done all you could." He thought she had done too much. It was why she wouldn't announce their engagement or set a date for their marriage. Since the age of fifteen she had cared for her mother as if she, Liz, were the mother, and Ellen was the child. And after Morgan Paige's death when Liz was eighteen, she had been both mother and father to Ellen.

"But what's the matter?" Liz was asking. "What do you want to tell me?"

"Not want to. Have to."

He saw the look of alarm in her bright eyes. Her soft full mouth quivered as she braced for the bad news she had come always now to expect . . . It had begun with a knock at the door ten years ago, with a few impersonal, slow-spoken, apologetic words. She would have heard, come running . . . Remembering that, he said, "The phone call was about John Vickery. He's dead."

Liz visibly relaxed. She lowered herself to the sofa and, looking across the room at a framed snapshot taken of her mother and father in the spring of their last good year together, she said, "So it's finally happened."

23

"Yes."

"And now only the Paiges are left."

"Not quite," Richard said, hesitating to go on.

The Paiges and the Vickerys. Meadowville's aristocrats and arbiters. Friends for generations before this one, when they had very nearly managed to destroy each other and themselves.

"Not quite?" she echoed. "What do you mean?"

This was the hard part. He took a deep breath. "Liz, I'm going to have to get in touch with Claude immediately."

A hot wave of color spread from her throat to her high cheekbones, and burned there like flame . . . Like the color of Maggie's hair. As it had been the summer she was seventeen . . . Hands clenched in her lap, Liz went rigid. Claude Vickery. The mention of his name could still do that to her after all the time that had passed.

"It's been over ten years, Liz," Richard said softly.

"Over? How can you say that? My mother still begs Maggie to come back, doesn't she? When she's not in bed, she's still sitting in her wheelchair, isn't she? Then how can you say it's over?"

"Liz . . ."

She cut in, her bitterness gouging sudden lines in her face. "Oh, don't say it. Mom's no better now than the day it happened. She's never going to be better. How can she? We'll live like this until her delusions completely destroy her mind. Or we'll live like this until she dies. You know that. And so do I."

"No, Liz. Dr. Detrick has always said the delusions might fade."

"They haven't. They won't."

"You can't be sure."

She shrugged his words away and plucked nervously at the

24

fabric of her riding trousers. "How can you get in touch with Claude? You don't know how to reach him. Nobody's heard from him in years. Not since he was put away. For all you know he's dead, too."

"He's alive. And I know how to reach him."

Her blue eyes burned. "You mean you know where Claude Vickery is?" Her face showed all her mixed feelings—rejection, disbelief, even fear—then hardened into a cold mask.

Richard nodded. "I'll call him as soon as I get home."

"But how do you know? And when did you find out? And why didn't you tell me?"

"The how and why is a long story. And I couldn't tell you before because I wasn't free to. Not until now. But would you have wanted me to? Even if I'd been able?"

"No," she said sharply. "I have no interest in Claude." But suddenly she found herself remembering a time when she had peered past the curtains in the living room window to watch Claude wait for Maggie at the foot of the drive. She remembered what Maggie had said about him in whispered confidences, part showing off to shock Liz, part just thinking aloud.

"He's a grown man now," Richard told her. "He's not the nineteen-year-old you knew."

"What will you call him for?" she demanded. "Just to tell him that John has died? He won't care. He never did. Why should it matter now?"

"There's more. John made a will."

"You drew it for him?"

Richard nodded. "Last year. And it's important that Claude come home."

"Home?" Color flooded her face again. "You mean come here? Back to Meadowville?"

"It's my responsibility to see that John's wishes are carried out. He made Claude his heir, if I could find him. And if Claude would come home."

"John's wishes," Liz said in a heated voice. "Damn them, and him, too." She pushed herself to her feet, and went on. "What about us? *Our* wishes? John's dead. It doesn't matter to him any more. But how about my mother? And me?"

Richard used the same words he'd used before. "It's over, Liz." He got up, drew her into his arms. For a moment Liz melted to him, her mouth soft, sweet, responsive to his kiss. But then she broke away.

"It isn't over. But do whatever you think you have to do," she said, and went into the kitchen.

As he was leaving he stopped to see Ellen Paige. She raised her head, smiled faintly. For an instant he saw the vague outline of how she used to look. Then it was gone.

"Leaving, Richard?"

"Something's come up. I won't be staying for dinner."

"Ah. I'm sorry. I always enjoy your visits so."

"I'll be back," he promised. Even though she saw him at least for a little while nearly every day, she seemed to need to pretend that each time was special.

She leaned toward him. "You know, Richard, Maggie always liked you."

He didn't answer. He couldn't . . . There had been a night when Maggie had opened her lips under his awkward kiss and he had tasted her thrusting tongue, and when she had bared her breasts to his fumbling hands. He'd imagined himself three-quarters of the way to heaven then. But it wasn't heaven at all, rather some kind of hell. For after that one time she seemed to forget his name, his face. He saw her with Red

Stanton, with Claude. With almost every boy in town . . .

"She's close by, Richard," Ellen said. "I can feel her. Maybe, if you allowed yourself to, you'd feel her, too."

He knew argument would only prolong it. It was useless for him to say, *The dead are dead, and that's the end of it.*

"She did always like you," Ellen told him.

"And I liked her," he answered.

"It'll happen, Richard. You'll see. Maggie will come back. She has to. It isn't over yet."

He made himself smile. "I'll see you tomorrow, Mrs. Paige."

She turned toward the window. "I'm glad. It's good for Liz to have company."

He got into his car, wondering how a woman could look sane, be normal in every way except for the ability to walk, and still believe that her Maggie could speak to her, come to her, from a ten-year-old grave.

The evening was cool, damp. A thin blood-red crescent of sun hung at the low ridge of hills that reared rounded peaks to the west. The long dark shadow of Dead Man's Bluff already lay across the town.

He drove slowly through the quiet streets, knowing he shouldn't waste time, but dreading the tasks that awaited him.

He had realized when John Vickery had first come to him that it would be difficult. Anything that involved the man turned out that way. He was opinionated, closed minded and set in his ways. He always had been. That had been part of the trouble between him and his brother Claude, Richard thought. Richard had even considered referring John to another attorney. But he hadn't been able to bring himself to do it. The man was so obviously ill even then. John was forty-four, Richard

27

knew, and looked sixty-four. His thin hair was gray, his face too, lips and eyes colorless, marked by the disease that would eventually kill him. He had been heavy when younger, granite in form as well as in manner and will. Now he was frail, but the granite was still in him, though Richard had been misled by his first few words. "I want you to make my will. I'm going to leave everything to Claude. The house and its lot. And all the other property I own."

Richard had thought that John had finally found that blood told after all, that he couldn't will what he owned to strangers, not when he had a living brother. But then John had said, "On two conditions." And Richard realized that John had never changed.

"If he's to claim it, he must come home to my funeral. I want him here to see me buried. And after that he must live here in Meadowville for at least two years."

"You've seen him? Spoken to him?" Richard asked, hoping his voice was calm and dispassionate as an attorney's should be, although the questions were asked as much out of old memories as present professional concern . . .

They had been friends once, he and Claude. Claude had been good to him, the new boy in town, the outsider, the son of a divorced traveling saleswoman who had settled in Meadowville because it was the center of her territory and who came home once a week, sometimes alone, and sometimes with a man she introduced as her cousin from the East. She had a lot of cousins from the East, Richard, and the town, soon understood. Her traveling job, and those cousins, had made it difficult for Richard. Only Claude understood his loneliness, because Claude, for other reasons, was lonely, too.

It wasn't until later that the two years difference between

28

them mattered. The age difference—and Maggie. At least that was what Richard had always tried to tell himself. But he knew better. There was more. He had needed so intensely to belong, to be accepted. He couldn't allow himself to be allied to an outcast. Not then. When Claude had needed defending, when he had needed at least one voice to speak up for him, Richard had been too vulnerable himself. But now he was older, stronger. . . .

"I don't know where Claude is," John had said. "I've not seen him or heard from him. Not since they locked him up. And I still don't want to."

"He was only a boy when it happened," Richard said.

"Nineteen," John answered. "Nineteen. A man. At least enough of a man not to go joyriding on the night his father was buried. Enough of a man to avoid even further disgracing the family name."

Richard hadn't answered. He could feel all the old bitterness filling the room. It wasn't a familial love that directed John. It was the same hate that had surrounded Claude from the day he was born. The same hate, but grown like a fungus on what Claude had done on the night of the day his father was put in his grave.

John didn't mention Dane Vickery, the embezzlement of the two hundred and fifty thousand dollars from the bank of which he was president, the unexplained confession that came before discovery, or the return of the money. But he thought of this, and not of Claude stumbling over the still-warm body, stumbling through the funeral, dazed, ashen faced . . .

"Enough of a man to stand up and face the music," John had continued. "Instead of cracking up and falling apart."

"The shock was too much for him. Maybe if he'd had

somebody . . . if they hadn't come at him so hard so fast . . . When he was so alone . . ."

"I was alone too," John had answered. "And I survived it." He went on, "You can find him if he's alive. And since I never heard differently, I think he must be."

"I'll start right away," Richard had said.

"You'll wait until I die. Then give yourself six months to find him. If you don't, the town gets all I have. If you do find him right away, and he comes back for my funeral and to live for two years, he has it all. And he'll have earned it, won't he?"

Richard knew that John was remembering the talk in the shops, the bars, at the country club. Dane Vickery, the big man in town, was a thief. How come he'd stolen that money? How come he'd given it back? And a coward too. Why hadn't he had the guts to face what he'd done? And then Claude . . .

"Suppose Claude can't come back? What if his work, or his life now . . . even his feelings . . ."

John's pallor seemed to deepen. "Too bad."

Richard hadn't asked for an explanation. He understood. John wanted Claude to live as John had lived. Hour by hour, day by day, walking the streets where Maggie Paige had once run and played and danced. Passing the desolate grounds of the Paige house. Sweating at the sudden sound of sirens in the dark or at a knock on the door after midnight. He wanted Claude to live, remembering, in the shadow of Dead Man's Bluff.

Richard had drawn up the will as directed, following John's instructions in every particular. He hadn't liked it, but he'd done it. Mindful of the mysterious grapevine of the town, he had bypassed June Stanton, who worked for him, and typed it himself in a slow hunt and peck, and locked it in his safe after John had signed it.

30

That day he had again asked John's permission to institute the search for Claude immediately, but John had been adamant. Richard was to wait until notified of John's death.

Richard wasn't sure whether John hoped that it would take longer than six months to locate Claude. He himself feared it might, but said nothing more, though the delay continued to rankle in him. He was bombarded at once by old loyalties and by old guilts. Six months wasn't enough time to give to locating a man who had been missing for ten years.

Within a month Richard had convinced himself that it would not be unethical to try to find Claude Vickery then, instead of waiting for leukemia to take John, as long as no one but he himself knew of his efforts, and if he were successful, knew where to reach Claude. For that reason ne undertook the task instead of giving it to a detective agency as he would normally have done.

It took him thirteen days of a two-week vacation. He went first to the last place that he knew Claude had been. The state mental hospital. It was only some five hundred miles from Meadowville. Once he had breached the wall of bureaucratic indifference it was easy to follow Claude's trail. Claude had made no effort to hide himself. He had been released, as cured, seven years earlier. He had gone as far from home as he could go. He settled in New York City, got a job as a delivery boy for a printing firm, went to art school at night, and ended up a successful comic-strip artist. His syndicated strip was signed only "Vick," and Richard knew he had seen it every Sunday when he read the metropolitan newspaper bussed in by dawn each week. Claude was even listed in the Manhattan phone directory under his own name.

So Richard had known exactly how to reach him, and done

31

nothing about it for just under a year . . .

Now, parked in front of his dark house, he glanced at his watch. A two-hour time difference. It would be nine-thirty in New York. Not too late to call.

He went slowly up the walk. It was becoming harder than ever to come home to the emptiness, to unlock the door on the unwelcoming silence. To poke his head into the dusty downstairs office and then go up the narrow steps to his equally dusty bachelor quarters. He wanted a wife and a home. More than anything he wanted Liz.

But she wouldn't let him share the responsibility for her mother. Somehow she managed on her father's pension, shrunken to a pittance now by inflation. Morgan Paige had been an honest man, an honest judge, and had left nothing else. Somehow she kept her sanity and sweetness through those moments when her mother pleaded for long-dead ears to hear her, long-shriveled lips to answer.

Once inside Richard put aside his familiar thoughts, telling himself that he'd find a way to deal with it all soon. He and Liz would marry, make a home, wherever it was, and build a life together.

Unconsciously, he jutted his square jaw, taking on the stubborn expression that he occasionally had in the courtroom. He was a big man, with sandy hair, and roughhewn features that would have made him look hard, except for his usual quizzical manner and a certain tentative squint to his gray eyes.

He hung his jacket over the back of his chair, loosened his tie. He found the Vickery file in his safe, and brought it back to his desk. As he picked up the phone he blessed the direct long distance system which gave him the privacy no one could

32

have relied on years before. He dialed 212, the exchange, and the rest of the number. Static on the line made him frown. But as the ring began, the noise faded. One ring. Two. He wondered if he would have to call again later. New York was probably a late-night city. He wondered what kind of life Claude lived. And then he heard the click, a breath. A deep voice said, faintly questioning, "Vickery."

"Claude?" Richard asked, and didn't wait. He knew. "Claude, this is Richard Braun. I'm calling from Meadowville. I have news for you about your brother John."

Another breath. A silence.

It would be startling, Richard thought. A sudden voice from the past. A voice. A name. The memories that they brought with them. Memories of a bitter childhood . . . Memories of Maggie.

Finally Claude spoke. "It's been a long time, hasn't it, Richard? You're calling about John, you say?"

His words, slow, even, unmarked by the old stammer, were therefore unfamiliar, although still recognizable by the deep voice. Richard tried to fit both to his recollection of Claude and couldn't. He seemed to be talking to a stranger.

"About John," Claude repeated.

"I'm sorry. He died this evening. He's had leukemia for about a year." Richard paused. There was no response so he hurried on. "I thought you'd better know right away."

Again there was silence. "Why?" Claude finally asked.

"You must be at the funeral."

"I must?"

Richard explained the first condition of the will, then said he was going to file the papers early Monday morning and wanted to discuss them with Claude. The funeral arrangements would be done in Meadowville, the burial Sunday afternoon.

"What's there to discuss?" Claude asked.

Richard explained the second condition. "There's more than you realize. The house and its land. Plus other property John amassed. It amounts to a small fortune now."

"I don't need John's money, thank you. I'm doing very well on my own. But who inherits if I say to hell with it?"

"The town."

Claude laughed mirthlessly. "That's my brother John all right."

"Will you be here?"

"I never thought of going back."

"I understand. But what John left is yours by right. And Claude . . ." Richard hesitated. "Claude, remember, what happened ten years ago is done."

"Yes," he said, his voice faintly questioning. "Yes. All right. I'll be in town before noon. On Sunday."

Richard suggested that Claude come to his house and asked if Claude remembered where it was.

There was a chuckle. "Sure I remember." And, referring to the past, "This time *you'll* be taking taking care of *me*, won't you?"

"It won't be necessary," Richard said. But he knew that Claude was right. This time it was he who was the stranger.

"Sunday," Claude said, and the connection was broken.

Richard put down the phone. He carefully replaced the Vickery file in the safe. He brushed a faint sheen of sweat from his forehead, and fixed himself a Scotch on the rocks. He sipped it while he talked to Dr. Detrick. He fixed another one before he called the memorial home to set up the arrangements. Discussing lot, limousine, minister and flowers, he remembered that he hadn't had anything to eat since his noon lunch. He had a third drink with a dry cheese sandwich.

He told himself that early the next day he would have to tell Liz that he had reached Claude and that Claude was coming home. She must have time to prepare herself and her mother. There was no telling how Mrs. Paige would react. Richard could only hope it wouldn't be too hard on her and on Liz. Monday, after the will was filed in the registry at the county seat, he'd be able to explain the rest of it.

Richard was beginning to wish he was the kind of man who could go out and get drunk. An itch of uneasiness was spreading through him. He wanted to hear conversation, even the dull talk he could hear in a bar. He wanted distraction, even if it was only too-loud country music. He wanted relief, even if it came only with the blurring of his senses.

But he knew he could drink all night, and nothing would happen. He'd still be himself. Damn it. What was he worried about? Ten years was a long time. The townspeople wouldn't remember. And if they did, they had more on their minds than Claude. Besides, what could they do?

From outside there came the sound of a car. He got to his feet and went to look.

Liz was walking up the path. She moved in her usual quick swinging walk. Lithe, graceful. Her slim body was high breasted, curved at the hip, voluptuous in its own way. He remembered her at fifteen. A tomboy. Good at tennis. A competent diver. An excellent swimmer. Always in jeans and shirts and sneakers. A late bloomer, who seemed awkward and even wan beside her sister Maggie. Maggie of the flaming hair and flashing eyes and seductive laugh. With time Liz had become beautiful, but had never known it. Nor had she ever learned that laugh . . .

He hurried down and threw open the door.

"I just couldn't stand it," she cried. "Not tonight. I got Mrs. Baldwin to come over and stay with mother for a few hours so I could be with you."

He grinned, forgetting his wish to be drunk, forgetting Claude Vickery, the will, the town. He led her inside.

It was later. The room was dark. They lay in each other's arms, their bodies warmed and softened by love.

She pressed her face into his bare shoulder, whispered, "It was so good. It was everything. For a little while. But now it has all come back. And I keep wondering what's going to happen to us. To you and me."

And he, answering, promised, "We'll make it happen the way we want it to. We'll be together, Liz. Soon."

CHAPTER 2

Claude pushed away the phone. Though the room was cool enough, his glasses slipped on his sweaty nose and his shirt stuck to his damp back. He grimaced and wiped his wet palms on his trousers.

From outside he heard the hoot of police cars, the wail of ambulances, the shrill sirens of fire engines. He lunged for the window to stare into the street below.

Then, annoyed with himself, he shrugged. It was nothing. He'd long been accustomed to these big-city sounds. They hadn't become alarm signals just because he'd been talking with Richard Braun.

Claude told himself everything was okay. Cool it. Never mind the pulses knocking in his temples. Forget the faint breathlessness. It mustn't bother him. All he had to do was wait it out. Soon it would go away. He'd at least learned that much over the years.

So John was dead. He was only forty-four. Few men died naturally at that age. But Claude knew it was a question that didn't really matter. He'd felt nothing for John alive, and could feel nothing for him now. For as long as Claude could remember it had been the same for John. His brother had known what it would mean for him to return to Meadowville.

Claude took off his glasses, closed his eyes and leaned his forehead against the cool windowpane.

He was a tall man, very thin, although he ate voraciously by long habit. He had a narrow face and deep-set brown eyes, with cheeks that were hollowed under prominent bones. His hair was dark and straight, haphazardly cut, with a single thick wing that fell across his high forehead. His shoulders were wide but slouched. He was ungainly somehow. When he walked it was in surges. A few quick steps, then a hitch. As if, always, something reached out to hold him back and he had to struggle against it to go on.

He felt the panic slowly fade out of him. He knew what had happened. Richard Braun had told him to go back to Meadowville, and Meadowville meant loud, suspicious, demanding voices coming at him through a fog of terror. But Meadowville also meant Maggie. And the only love he'd ever known.

He straightened, swung away from the window. He had told Richard that he didn't need John's money. And it was true. He could turn his back on it, on Richard's call. He could tell John, the will, to go to hell, and forget that he'd ever had a phone call from Meadowville.

But, suddenly, he wanted to go. He knew now that it was the unfaced wanting that had made him agree so quickly. He had waited all these years. Finally he was ready. He wanted to see the places where he and Maggie had gone, to ride along Dead Man's Bluff, remembering. He needed to be again where they had been together.

That was why he'd told Richard he'd be there in time for the funeral. That was why he wouldn't change his mind. He *wanted* to go. And why not? He was twenty-nine now. A grown man. A successful and self-sufficient man. He was no longer a lost nineteen-year-old. He'd put in all he had, all he was, to come this far. It couldn't be for nothing.

He started for the phone, then hurried to the pullman kitchen. He was ravenously hungry. Although he'd had a big dinner, he felt as if he hadn't eaten for a week. He fixed two cold roast beef sandwiches.

Carrying them with him, he went back to the phone. He'd said he'd be in Meadowville by Sunday noon. And he would be. But meanwhile he had things to do. . . .

The headlights danced, sliding ahead over the sharp teeth of the rocks and flickering in the August-dry leaves of the live oaks and birches. It was a moonless night. The shadows formed black walls along the invisible edges of the curving road. In the valley below there was the faint glow of distant windows. The lit spire of a church marked the town he was leaving. For good. Forever. He couldn't wait to get away. Finally. At long last. Forever.

Beside him, Maggie tossed her bright head and laughed. "It's like flying, and I love it. Go faster, Claude."

Her eyes, which were by day the violet of a summer desert sky at late afternoon, now sparkled midnight black. Her curly hair floated around her face like a gleaming veil.

He turned and smiled at her, and she smiled back.

"Like loving," he said. And his stammer was gone. The curse that had afflicted him for as long as he could remember, the curse that tied his tongue and made him seem stupid, the curse that had bound him in loneliness, he knew was now gone for good. It would never wrack him again.

She leaned her head on his shoulder, snuggling close. "It was always you. More than Red. More than Richard. Maybe it didn't always seem that way to you, Claude. But that's how it was."

"You're with me," he told her. "That's all I care about."

He wasn't thinking ahead. It would work out. He had saved four hundred dollars. He would get a job. They'd find a place to live. They'd be together. And nobody would be able to get between them, or pull them apart, or do anything to hurt them.

Her hand caressed his thigh as the car labored up the hump of Dead Man's Bluff through the tunnel of black shadows. The road narrowed and swung in a hairpin to the ridge, and he slowed even more. But, suddenly, the rear end swung out. The wheel became his adversary, whipping in his fingers. He fought back with all his strength, hearing Maggie scream. *No, no.*

There was a jolt. A spine-wrenching, teeth-rattling jerk. The road, the hump, the world fell away from under them. They spun through the night, flung briefly together, then torn apart, while he heard his own shout and the thin high pitch of her unending cry.

They plowed into thunder. Dust rising. Leaf and limb spinning. A volcano of noise and debris. Dark fell on him, blinding weight. It slid away on brilliance. He lay half-buried in the furrow dug by his flung body. There was crackling, hissing. A strange orange glow. He staggered up.

A pine made a blazing torch against the sky. At its base, crumpled, aflame and on its side, lay the car.

He stumbled into enveloping heat. "Maggie! Maggie, where are you?"

No sign of her on the roiled earth.

"Maggie!"

No answer.

Embers on his cheeks, hair, clothes. Small licks of scattered pain.

"Maggie!"

His throat was raw. His hands were seared. Eyes streaming, he staggered closer still.

Something moved at the open window. Fingers waved at him. He lunged through fire and heat and leaned nearer. He reached through the window and pulled at her. "Maggie! Oh, God, help me, Maggie!" Her arms went around his neck. She clung to him, wordlessly screaming as flame breathed on the veil of her hair.

He pulled, dragged. The car held her fast. And she held him.

He fought to free her. But at the last he fought to free himself. Under the whip of fire he broke out of her encircling arms, and staggered back and fell. As he dropped into darkness once again, he heard the blast of the explosion . . .

It hurt. The touch on his shoulder was pain. He jerked, fought against it.

A voice said, "Sir, are you all right?"

He opened his eyes into a direct blue gaze. A peaked blue cap sat aslant on blond curls. He heard, "Sir? Are you all right?" This time it was insistent.

He didn't know where he was or what was wrong. There was no firelight now, no sound of exploding gasoline. The slim, well-manicured hand on his shoulder was in no way the grip of smoking sinewy arms around his neck. Having shaken him gently awake, it was withdrawn.

Slowly, reality came to him. The plane. The present. And

then memory. The accident on Dead Man's Bluff. The past. It had been what he slept with for years after he'd slowly, laboriously and fearfully found himself again. When the intervals between the dream began to lengthen he knew he was finally free. When the dream faded, he had rejoiced. But Richard's call, the return to Meadowville, had brought it back.

"A nightmare," he croaked, and breathed deeply. "A nightmare. Sorry."

The blue eyes gazed at him a moment longer. Then the blond head nodded. The stewardess smiled and withdrew.

Claude wiped his damp face with his handkerchief, polished his metal-rimmed glasses and shifted and stretched his long, tense body until it found ease again.

Gradually his quick breathing slowed, and the dream images faded. He was on the plane. In a little while it would land in Chicago. He would make the change for the last short leg to St. Louis. There, at Avis, a car would be waiting for him.

He was going home. That explained the dream. It was the first time in years that he'd had it, though his memory of Maggie was as much a part of him as his bones and flesh and blood. His love for his lost Maggie was the same as when it was new, wondrous, the only love he'd ever known. Still, it was years since he'd dreamed of the night they'd gone flying up the hump of Dead Man's Bluff, and spun away ablaze, and he'd come to, fighting her fiery arms from around his neck . . .

There was a nudge at his arm, a small cough. The woman beside him said, "I thought you were having a stroke."

He turned his head. She was middle-aged, small, with ridges of powder in the creases on her face. "I'm sorry I disturbed you," he said.

"Worried me is more like it. I saw it happen once. It scared me. I didn't want it to happen again."

He unhooked his seat belt and escaped to the lavatory. There he washed his face, ran a comb through his hair. One dark lock immediately fell into an unruly curve on his forehead. His eyes stared back at him from the small mirror with a faint look of surprise.

He was on his way home, and still couldn't quite believe it. Not that he was committed. He could spend a few hours there and then leave. He didn't have to go back to stay. Not unless he decided he wanted to. It was as he'd told Richard—John's money wasn't that important. But it was rightfully his, Claude thought. He was the last Vickery.

When the warning light blinked red, he went back to his seat, strapped himself in. The woman beside him cleared her throat, preparing to resume her tale.

He didn't want to hear any more, to know if the man had lived or died from his stroke. Claude kept his face resolutely turned away from the woman until the swoop for landing and the roar of the retrogrades forced her to keep her silence.

When the plane landed, and its doors opened, he was first off, leaving her and his dream, far behind.

There was a sign. He slowed to look at it. Meadowville. Population 31,000. The town was still shrinking, he thought, but it didn't surprise him. It had always been a backwater. Ten years ago, when he was nineteen, the Viet Nam War was accelerating. Richard Nixon was in the White House. Hair and beards were long, and jeans were the uniform. He'd come home after his freshman year and seen that Meadowville was unaffected.

Nothing had changed, not his father or his brother John.

Claude was still the unwanted stranger he had been when he was born and his mother died.

He didn't know what Meadowville was now, but he knew he wasn't the same Claude Vickery who had returned home that long-ago summer. Of that old self there remained only his memory of Maggie, and his love for her.

And he felt close to her here, driving past Paige Park where they had walked together, seeing the familiar landmarks of Main Street.

It hurt. But it was good, too. Still, he was relieved when he saw the Braun property. He slowed the car and parked. He smoothed back the single lock of hair that had fallen across his forehead and adjusted his glasses.

As he got out of the car a small black cat shot from under a bush and streaked across the cracked sidewalk with two angry blue jays swooping at its head. Claude knew how the cat felt. He clapped his hands and scared the birds away.

Richard came out to meet him. They shook hands, exchanged greetings and went inside.

The room was different from what Claude remembered. Where was the faded straw rug? The broken easy chairs? What had happened to Richard's mother? Claude decided not to ask.

Richard, however, explained about the office, the bachelor quarters upstairs. He didn't mention that his mother had married one of her so-called cousins and moved to San Francisco, leaving the house for Richard. He got coffee, brought it in and served Claude.

While Claude drank it, Richard told him that John had never married, had been a recluse. Claude only nodded, unwilling to pretend to a grief he didn't feel.

After explaining in detail the conditions set by John's will,

Richard said, "Regardless, the estate is morally yours. And you should have it."

"You're worried I'm going to refuse, aren't you?"

"I don't think you should decide quickly."

"I thought I'd leave tomorrow morning after the funeral."

"I don't need an immediate answer," Richard said.

"I'll think about it," Claude said, closing the subject. But he already knew what he was going to do. He went on, "You look pretty much the same."

"Just ten years older."

"So do I."

"No. You're different, Claude. You've changed."

"Maybe." But Claude knew it was true. He wasn't the boy he had been when they took him away . . . In a white camisole. Lashed to an unpadded cot. The last thing he'd seen before they closed the ambulance doors on him was John's ashen, hating face. That was the last thing he saw when his mind turned off. And it was what he remembered first when he began to see light again. First John. And then Maggie . . .

Claude and Richard made small talk about living in New York. Richard asked if Claude had married, and when he said that he hadn't, told Claude that he and Liz Paige were going together.

"Maggie's younger sister." It was the first time the name had been spoken. And for the first time Claude felt the muscles in his throat tighten. There was the hint of a coming stammer. He pulled a deep breath in, let it out. "I remember her."

A small silence fell. Neither of the two men spoke until Richard looked at the wall clock, then got up, saying they might as well get started. A limousine waited outside.

Claude raised his brows. "You're doing it up right."

"John's instructions were very detailed," Richard said. Inside, leaning back against the plush seat, he went on. "I want you to be prepared. You're going to see everyone, I suppose. The town's going to turn out."

"Because of me as well as John," Claude said flatly.

"Probably."

"I'm ready," Claude said.

"The Paiges will be there. Liz. Mrs. Paige."

Claude nodded. Maggie's mother. Sister. "And what about Judge Paige?"

"He died of a massive stroke seven years ago."

Claude said nothing . . . Seven years ago he had been released from the institution. He had gone straight to New York. The therapist and social worker had both tried to get him to go home. But he'd refused. There'd been nothing for him in Meadowville. There'd been nothing and no one to draw him back . . .

"I'd better warn you," Richard was saying, "Liz's mother has changed greatly. She was ill. When she recovered she was crippled. And since then, sometimes, not always, you understand, but sometimes her mind . . ."

"What are you beating around the bush about?"

"She has delusions, Claude. She talks about Maggie."

Claude nodded but didn't speak.

When the limousine drew up before the memorial home, Richard asked, "Do you want to see John before the coffin is closed?"

"No." Claude followed as Richard led the way. It was as he had said. Now Richard was taking care of *him*.

The room was quiet, filled only with the scent of flowers.

Soft tuneless music played in the background. Claude took a chair. There were stirrings from the chapel, whispers. Richard hovered protectively close by. But suddenly Claude was uncomfortable, even frightened. He wished he hadn't come, and wondered why he had. Damn John's money, he thought. And damn John.

People wandered in. Faces blurred, but familiar. They looked at him, hesitating. Looked at him, stared and weighed him.

Claude asked himself what he was doing there, why he had come. He pulled off his glasses, polished them and set them back on his nose.

Richard said something but he didn't catch the words. When he looked up again he saw that the crowd had moved aside, and Richard was going to the door.

Framed there, as if caught in a picture, sat Mrs. Paige. Liz stood behind her, white faced, unsmiling.

A sudden hush fell. Every eye in the room centered on Claude. He felt as if he were being stabbed by multiple knives. Thick hot emotion swelled in his chest. Fear. Shame. A quick gush of tears rose up behind blinking lashes. He thought of Maggie, of how he had loved her.

Slowly he unfolded his long thin body. He rose, forcing himself from the chair to cross the room in his slouching walk, with his head thrust forward, the dark lock hanging over his forehead. Inside he was cringing. What would Mrs. Paige say? Do? And Liz? He hadn't thought ahead to this. How he would feel. How they would feel. He'd only thought of Maggie.

Mrs. Paige held out a thin hand. "Claude, I'm glad to see you again," she said gently. "I'm glad you've finally come home." A light burned far back in her lavender eyes. "Now I'm more sure than ever that Maggie will come back too."

"Oh, mom," Liz cried, "Please, please, this isn't the time."

CHAPTER 3

A murmur of muted approval followed Liz's words. No one wanted Ellen Paige to talk of Maggie now.

Ellen's thin icy fingers squeezed Claude's hand then released it. She raised faded eyes to Liz. "I'm sorry, dear."

Claude tried to speak, but his throat was frozen. Closed. Tight. So dry it felt stuffed with cotton. He was choking for air. For words. It was like when he was a boy and speech was his enemy. He waited, fighting back the need to answer too quickly. Hurrying was wrong, he knew, and to be pressured was to stammer. He held himself in check, aware of sharp curious glances, eyes that stabbed questioningly at his face. They'd be remembering what had happened . . . Maggie . . . They'd think of how he'd been crazy once. They'd maybe think he was crazy still. He didn't care. He wasn't going to stammer.

At last, after a long pause, when he was certain he was safe, he spoke. "How are you, Mrs. Paige?" A stupid question. He knew by looking at her how she was. Aged too soon. Sick. Destroyed. But what else was there to say? Only the truth. He said quietly, "I'm sorry. For everything."

Liz gasped.

Richard's hand clasped Claude's shoulder.

But Ellen Paige nodded acceptance of his words. "How am I? You see me as I am." She smiled faintly. "I'm not the woman I used to be."

No, he thought. She was no longer the cool-eyed woman who had been Maggie's mother. Friendly, but a little distant, and then, at the end, the enemy who would have kept them apart.

He turned to Liz, said her name softly, searching her blue eyes and rigid face for a sign of the friendliness that wasn't there. He recalled her as a quiet girl, pale in Maggie's sunshine. Now Liz was beautiful—but with no sign of Maggie in her. Hair chestnut instead of flaming red, eyes a vivid flashing blue instead of violet and laughing, body curved but taller, slimmer, harder. He wondered at his disappointment. There had only been one Maggie. There would never be another . . .

Liz nodded at him, but didn't speak. She didn't trust her words.

She had been in a daze of anger ever since Richard had told her that Claude was returning for John's funeral. She was angry at Richard for calling him, and angry at Claude for coming. But at the root of her anger was fear. Fear that Claude's presence would only make more real a past that was gone.

"It's been a long time, hasn't it?" he said to Ellen Paige.

"Yes. But it's over now. I feel it. I'm sure." Her faded eyes had become bright with exaltation. It had been a long time since she had heard her daughter's voice, seen her daughter's face. Ellen felt as if the chill of years was slowly lifting. Claude brought warmth where there'd been no warmth for her. Hope where there'd been only small hope. He brought the possibility of expiation . . . She reached to touch his hand again. "Come to see me, Claude. I mean it. Please come."

Whispers spread through the hushed room. There was the embarrassed shuffling of feet. A rustle of movement. The swift exchange of knowing glances.

Claude understood. If anyone had the right to a grievance against him, then she did. But she seemed not to remember that.

Liz whispered, "Mom . . ." And stopped herself. What was there to say that wouldn't make it worse?

"Claude knows," Ellen Paige said brusquely,

"Of course." He knew that seeing him brought Maggie back for her. Just as being here brought Maggie back for him. It was why he'd come.

Richard drew him away, saying that the services were about to begin. There'd be time, later, to speak more with Mrs. Paige, with Liz. And with the others.

They were only moments in the chapel. The minister explained that John Vickery had requested that there be no eulogy, and read the Twenty-third Psalm.

A twenty-seven-car procession followed the flower-decked hearse to the cemetery.

The large group gathered around the open grave. The coffin was lowered slowly. There was a squeal of leather straps, a jolt. The minister winced, waited.

Except for one quick glance toward the Paige family lot, where he knew Maggie was buried, Claude kept his eyes fixed on the ground. They were all staring at him, he knew. He could feel their glances. They weren't here for John. They were here to stare at him, weigh him. He was changed. But they were the same.

The minister finished the reading in a quiet voice, and gently closed the Bible.

Claude turned away, glad that it was over.

Claude and Richard reached the house before the others. It was exactly as Claude remembered it, except that the white paint was blistered and a green shutter hung crooked on a broken hinge. And inside there were more voices, more bustle and life than he'd seen in it throughout the years of his growing up.

Richard had had a caterer bring in a small lunch. There was a coffee urn perking on the polished mahogany table. There were baskets of rolls and plates of relishes set among platters of sliced ham and turkey. The waiters made last-minute adjustments to the napkins and silver. A bartender polished glasses.

When Claude had known this living room it had been silent, the drapes always closed against light. In one chair his father, Dane, would sit. In another sat John. They would hold newspapers in front of their faces, and wouldn't notice when he came in. They paid no attention when he left. It was a house of perpetual mourning. Claude was raised by a succession of housekeepers who soon moved on without leaving a trace. There had been no mention of his mother. It was as if he'd never had one. When he was old enough to wonder, to ask, his questions went unanswered.

He learned from one of the transient housekeepers, when he was about eight, that his mother had been named Clara and that she had died at his birth. It was then that he finally began to understand. It was *his* fault. His father and John blamed him for Clara's death. They looked at him and mourned her. They hated him when they remembered her. There was no way to change their minds, to win them, to earn their love.

He had never been a lovable little boy. He was skinny and wore glasses, and had a bad stammer. Ignored, he ended up shrinking into himself. He hid in books. He began to do small sketches. He waited passionately to grow up. He waited, longing for love.

The summer he was nineteen and home from college, he rediscovered Maggie Paige. She had always been pretty, but in his absence at school she had become beautiful. She was always at the center of a group of boys, laughing with them, belonging to none of them. Seventeen. Joyful. Greedy for life. She became his first love . . . his only love.

He worked days at Willie Harker's service station, which earned him Red Stanton's enmity. Red wanted the job himself. Before that, when Red noticed Claude at all, he had been openly contemptuous. But Claude didn't care. He had his Maggie.

They would ride up to Dead Man's Bluff and picnic under the stars. They walked in the sun-drenched meadows. She would read while he painted under the live-oak trees. By summer's end he knew he wouldn't leave her.

He was trying to think what to do, when a horn blared at him from a blue and white gas island in the station, and Red yelled, "Hey, Claude, hear the news?"

He shrugged, but Willie Harker said, "Go get him, Claude."

Red's hair was close cropped then. He wore a stained skivvy shirt. He leaned from the car window. "I guess you haven't heard." He was plainly enjoying himself when he went on,

53

"Your old man's in big trouble. He's probably going to prison."

Speechless, Claude stared at Red.

Red grinned. "News to you, hunh? It's what I'd already figured. You're too dumb to catch on."

"Catch on to what?"

"What your old man's been up to. That's what." Red gunned the motor and shot out of the station.

Willie came over. "What was that about?" he asked.

"I don't know," Claude had said. "I think he's gone crazy." He dismissed the conversation.

Later that day Claude learned that Red hadn't gone crazy . . .

When he got home he was thinking about Maggie, how he couldn't leave her to go back to school. He tried to plan, but his thoughts went in circles. He had to return to school. It was what his father wanted. But he couldn't leave Maggie. He was trying to figure out how to put it into words so he could explain it to his father that night, that last night, when he went into the house. That was how he thought of it. That last night. An accurate description. The last night of one life, and the beginning, although he didn't know it then, of another.

The house was as quiet as always. He turned, closed the door gently. The grandfather clock ticked. A fly buzzed at the window. For a long, still moment he remained in the foyer. Not because he sensed anything amiss. Only because he needed to brace himself to talk to his father.

But it was no good just standing there. He knew that the sooner he tried, the better he would feel. As he went down the hall, he heard the grandfather clock chime six times. He knocked, pushed open the library door. His mouth and tongue opened, but he choked.

54

Finally he got the words out, stammering. "Father, I have to talk to you about something important."

But the effort had been wasted. Too late, he saw that the room was empty. His father's chair was vacant. The desk top was clear of papers.

Claude started to back from the room. He was disappointed at the delay. He was relieved not to have to face his father's anger yet. At the threshold, looking over his shoulder, he paused. There was a shadow under the desk. A shadow that somehow had a familiar form.

He was suddenly frightened. He lunged around the desk and there, between it and the window, he found Dane Vickery. His father lay on the floor, a gun near his outstretched hands. Blood matted his hair, formed a puddle under his cheek.

Claude froze where he stood, the rumblings of an old terror echoing through him. His father had never been able to stand the sight of him. Claude had always known that some day, some how, his father would leave him. It had finally happened.

With a cry of pain he ran for the phone . . .

Now a door slammed. Claude blinked, and returned to the present.

Red Stanton came toward him, a long, slanting grin on his mouth. "Long time no see. So you finally came home, Claude. I wondered if you ever would."

"How are you?" Claude asked.

"Ten years older and ten years smarter," Red answered.

He was a big man. Though the same age as Claude, he looked older. His face was pitted, scarred. His hair was nearly shoulder length, held neatly in place by a green Indian headband at the forehead. His eyes were pale gray. The end of a tattooed snake showed beneath his right shirt cuff when he moved his wrist. Behind him stood a small blond girl. He reached back and pulled her forward. "This is June. My wife." He grinned down at her. "You've heard me talk about Claude Vickery, haven't you?"

As she stared at him, Claude wondered briefly what Red had said that made June look at him so blankly. "Hello, June. I hope you like Meadowville."

She gave him an empty smile, pushed thin fingers through her short curls.

"She works for Richard Braun," Red said.

"Typing. Answering the phone," she told Claude. "Whatever he wants me to do."

She had a funny sing-song voice, and when she spoke she kept shooting glances at Red, as if expecting comment or instruction from him.

Red laughed. "Not *whatever* he wants you to do, dummy."

Her eyes widened. "Well, I mean, in business. You know." She looked to Claude for help.

He didn't know what to say. "Sure. I know what you mean."

"Going to stay in town long?" Red asked.

"I don't know," Claude said. He didn't intend to tell anybody about his affairs until he was settled in his own mind.

"Not much for you in this town," Red went on.

"I guess not," Claude agreed. He excused himself, wanting to get away from Red. He was hungry. When he had finished stacking his plate, and had stepped away from the table, Red appeared again at his elbow.

"You're looking good, Claude. You've made it, haven't you?" Red didn't wait for an answer before adding another question. "And where've you been all this time?"

"What about you?" Claude asked.

"Plenty of places. Viet Nam, for a while. I guess you stayed out of that because of the funny farm." Red's mouth slanted briefly. "Then I was just traveling around. Seeing the country."

Claude was glad to see Richard push Ellen Paige into the room. He set his plate down, nodded at Red, and walked away quickly.

He went over to Ellen Paige. "Let me get you something to eat."

"Liz's at the table now." Mrs. Paige smiled up at him. "I saw you talking to Red. Don't mind what he says."

"I never did."

"Oh, that's not what I mean," she said hastily. She knew about when Red had called Claude "Four eyes," because he wore glasses, and "Duckfoot," because of his awkwardness, and "Triple tongue," because of his stammer. But that wasn't what she had in mind. "I was thinking of now . . . now, you see. He came home so surly from the war and wherever else he went afterwards. Yes, surly and sour. And with that poor girl he married along the way." Ellen sighed. "People make mistakes that haunt them forever." Her words were whispered. Her eyes were on Red, but she was speaking of herself. "And then," she went on, "and then, for the rest of their lives they pay. They do the best they can, but they keep on paying and there's no end to it."

Liz thrust a plate of food into her mother's hands. "You'd better eat, mom."

"You've hardly changed, Liz," Claude said.

She looked at him, didn't smile. "I don't know if I should take that as a compliment. I'm ten years older than when you last saw me. Something should have happened since then."

"But you don't look that much older."

"You've learned flattery along the way," she said dryly.

He searched her face, again looking for some sign of Maggie. They were sisters. There ought to be something, he thought, at least a small indication that they were related. A shadow, a nuance, an expression. A slant of eye. Curve of lips. A touch of color. Something that hinted of shared blood. He couldn't find it. It was depressing to acknowledge the absence.

"How long will you be here?" Liz asked.

"I . . . I don't know yet."

"You have to get back to work, I guess."

He knew by the hope in her voice that she wanted him out of Meadowville. And Red Stanton was staring at him, a slanted grin on his mouth, and June Stanton was eyeing him as if he were a dangerous animal. Dr. Detrick was also watching Claude speculatively. They were all wondering about him, and remembering.

He said softly, "Liz, I was always so sorry. I wanted to tell you, your folks . . . but it happened so fast. One thing, then another. I never had time . . ."

"Don't talk about it," she said sharply. She paused for a deep breath. "I have to tell you, Claude . . . seeing you has upset my mother. Please stay away from her. For her sake. And mine."

He didn't know what to say.

Liz looked at him. "You see how she is."

"Frail. Obviously she's not well."

"And crazy," Liz said quietly.

Quick heat filled him. It was what they had said about him. And, he supposed, it must have been true. At least for a while. But Ellen Paige didn't seem crazy. She smiled, shook hands, made polite conversation. Finally he asked, "What are you talking about?"

"What she said. About Maggie's coming back."

"But it's only a way of speaking," he protested.

"It's a lot more than that," Liz said soberly.

When the others had finally gone, Richard asked. "What do you think, Claude?" There were things, Richard thought, that he ought to have done for Claude years ago. It was too late for those things. But this was something he could do for him now. "If you could work here . . ."

"I can work anywhere." Claude smiled faintly. "And have." He had once drawn behind locked doors and barred windows, aware of being watched through one-way glass. He had worked in a grocery store back room, breathing the odor of onions and rotten potatoes.

But he was thinking of how he had almost begun to stammer again. Of the cool, unwelcoming look in Liz's blue eyes. Of Red Stanton's slanted grin. Of how Willie Harker had stared at him, rubbing the dark bristles on his jaw, and how he had whispered to Vernon Meese, whose blond hair was thinner and whose stomach was bigger than Claude remembered. He was thinking of the speculation in Dr. Detrick's round face. Remembering them, and the others, he told himself he didn't care, and felt his throat tightening again.

When Richard offered to put him up for the night, Claude looked at the grandfather clock, the mahogany table. He shook his dark head. "If I come back to stay it'll have to be here." He was actually thinking, *When I come back to stay . . .*

"You could buy another house. If you wanted to. It might be hard to live here."

"It *was* hard. Then. But not any more. I'm not the boy I was."

"No," Richard agreed.

"I'll stay here. I'll call you tomorrow and let you know what I'm going to do." Actually he was just giving himself a little more time. He already knew what his answer would be.

Claude walked slowly through the empty house. It was good, now, to be alone. Leaving a trail of lights behind him, he paused on the threshold of the library. Then he pushed the door open and went in.

Two standing lamps glowed when he flicked the switch. He looked at the desk. It was as bare topped as he had remembered it all these years. But there was no shadow beneath it, no body sprawled behind its massive bulk. . . .

He had called John at the bank, choking out the words, then Dr. Detrick. He had waited through what seemed no longer than an indrawn breath. Outside, sirens wailed. Tires squealed. Red dome lights blinked angry signals in the evening sun . . .

Now he shrugged, turned off the memory and the lamps at the same time, and continued on his passage. The familiar kitchen was more dingy than he recalled it, though it had been dingy back then, too. The hallway, hung with old photographs of the Greek Islands and views of the harbor of Rio de Janeiro. They had always been there.

Upstairs he looked briefly into John's room, then went into his own. It was the same as when he had left it, except for the curtains, which were more faded now. The bookcase, tilted on one broken leg, was still full of the volumes he had read. On the wall there was tacked a small watercolor, unframed, unsigned, that he had done that last summer he was home.

He looked at it for a long time before he found sheets and

changed the linen. Then he went to stand at the window for a last cigarette before getting into the freshly made bed.

There was so much he didn't remember well, or remember at all. But there were some moments he had never forgotten. . . .

He had climbed up the rocky hillside, leaving the smoldering ruin of the car behind him. Staggering on the road, he had yelled hoarsely into the dark. He had screamed, "Maggie! Maggie!" He didn't know how much time passed while he cried for her to come back to him.

A truck came. Soon it was a repetition of two days before when he had called first John, then Dr. Detrick. But this time he was on Dead Man's Bluff. In the dark. With his flesh seared and his heart broken. Sirens wailed; police cars hooted; red dome lights swung in angry arcs.

Shivering, weeping, stammering, he had managed to tell them before he collapsed.

Then there was morning light on pale green walls. His throat wrapped in greasy gauze. Judge Paige stood at his bedside, face grim, eyes accusing. The police. Dr. Detrick. The questions began.

He told them exactly how it had been. Exactly. Everything. As he remembered it. But from the beginning. He started with the day of his father's death.

Dane Vickery's name was disgraced.

Claude had seen it in the eyes of men who had been the older man's friends all their lives. They came, but not to mourn him. There were wry twists to their mouths. Whispers passed back and forth. What Claude didn't actually hear, he could imagine. *Playing at being straight all his life. Hah! A thief. That's what he was. Even if he did turn the money back. Could*

61

have wrecked the bank. Wrecked the whole damn town. And why? That's what I'd like to know. Why?

Ellen Paige was there, her face as rigid as marble, deathly pale under the loops of her auburn hair. Her long pale fingers writhed nervously in the folds of her black dress. Her eyes, when they briefly touched Claude, seemed to be asking *Why*, too. And it was the same for Judge Paige. Even his father's closest friend seemed to ask the same question.

In his heart, Claude knew the answer. Dead Clara. And living Claude. His father had tried all those years to put up with him, living with the reminder of the woman he had lost in Claude's birth. Dane had tried. But it got to be too much. He didn't want to live any more. Because Claude was born. Now, when it was too late, he felt for his father a sympathy, a love, he had never before known.

But he listened silently to the whispers, choking back the defense of his father, choking back his guilt and grief. They wouldn't want to hear the truth. They only wanted to tear Dane down.

Played at being the big shot. And look where it's led him. Remember the time I asked for an extension on the mortgage? And when I needed a loan to rebuild the barn? And all the time, there he was, stealing from the bank.

Hate was in those whispers, in the cold, assessing way those hard eyes looked at John, and at Claude himself.

The same day that his father died, John had resigned from the bank. Because he'd known he had to, although the bank had been Vickery's Bank for so many years.

And that same day, when the house was quiet again, Claude went to look for Maggie. He found her walking in her backyard, as if she'd known he would come. She'd said, "I'm sorry, Claude."

"Are you going to turn against me too?" he'd asked desperately. "Are you, Maggie?"

"What? Why should I? Why should anybody?"

"My dad."

She shrugged her slim shoulders, swung her flaming hair back from her face. "What your dad did is nothing to me, Claude."

"It might be." He stopped because he didn't know how to say it.

But she understood, as she had always understood him. "It'll blow over. And besides, it's not your fault. It doesn't change us."

"But it will."

"No," she said and smiled. "You'll see. If I don't want them to, they'll never change my mind. Nobody can. Ever. Not if I don't want them to."

He thought of her mother's rigid face and questioning eyes, of her father's grim expression. He didn't mention them. He said, "Everybody's saying my father's a crook, Maggie. John's already quit the bank."

"I don't care."

"But I do. I won't be able to stand it. I'm going to have to get out of here, I think." He'd wanted to anyway. He'd been planning to when his father killed himself, had walked into the library that night to tell his father what he intended to do.

"You mean you're going back to school?"

"Not school. I doubt I'll be able to go anyhow. No, I mean

to go away. Find work. Begin to live, and paint, and do what I want to do."

She had put her arms around him. "Claude . . . listen . . . what about me?"

"You're the only thing I don't want to leave behind. That was what made me see I have to go. They'll keep us apart from now on. And I can't stand that. I don't want to leave you, Maggie. But what else can I do?"

"Don't leave me."

"What?"

"Don't leave me." She pressed against him. The small curved body that he knew so well was then almost a part of his own. "I'm tired of being a little girl. Even if that's how they treat me. I want to grow up now. I want to live too."

"Maggie, are you sure?"

"I'll pack. I'll be ready. You just tell me when."

Judge Paige didn't believe it. He didn't even want to hear it. Over Claude's whispering voice, he had shouted, "You were joyriding on the day your father was buried. Joyriding! And now my Maggie's dead!"

And then, the police had come at him. "You were drunk, weren't you? That's why it happened!" And, "What were you on? Pot? Hash? What poison were you taking?" There were quiet and halfhearted protests from Dr. Detrick. John had said nothing.

Claude heard a lot of talk he didn't understand. When the room was empty and quiet again he lay still and thought of Maggie. That afternoon a nurse came. She helped him dress. Without speaking or explaining, she led him into the hall. The police were waiting. Men he knew only by face. They shoved him into an unmarked car. In a little while he was behind bars.

By then he knew that something terrible was happening to him. Something more terrible than the bars. He found that he couldn't speak any more. At first he'd tried a few stammering questions which no one had answered. But soon the stammer had frozen in his throat, blocking it. He could hear, but not as well as he was used to. He could see, but through a thickening mist. His arms, legs were beginning to be heavy, as if the controlling muscles had suddenly been stretched too far. His breath slowed.

Time passed, and he didn't know it. He remembered only one thing more. A terrifying moment when he was wrapped in a camisole, tied to an unpadded stretcher, and shoved into an ambulance. And John, white faced, hating him, watched while they closed the doors. . . .

Later, much later, he learned the rest of it. Voluntary manslaughter charges had been filed against him. Reckless driving. Third-degree homicide. But all charges were dropped by the following day, after Dr. Detrick had seen him. They'd called the doctor when they found Claude curled on his cot, unable to see or hear or speak. The doctor had made the necessary arrangements. Claude was sent to the mental institution.

Claude was there for three years, the first one still a blank, perhaps always to be. He'd fought his way back from that no-man's-land slowly. Therapy had brought him the rest of the way. Therapy, his art, and his own determination.

No one had come to see him, written to him, inquired about him. He was on his own then.

Just as he was on his own now.

He pressed out his cigarette, sighed. Suddenly he wanted to run away, he wanted to get into his rented car and drive as fast as he could and as far as he could from Meadowville.

He fought the feeling back. He clenched sweaty hands on the windowsill and hung on as tight as he could. Meadowville was home. He had every right to be here. He had the right to the money John had left, to this house and all it held, to his memories of Maggie. He told himself to relax.

The mockingbirds rustled in the eaves. They uttered brief trills before they went still.

Below, from the corner of his eyes, he saw a moving figure in the shadows of the garden. He swung his head around quickly. For an instant he saw it clearly, then it seemed to flicker away. Small, slim but curved. With an aureole of gleaming hair. Maggie. And as he remembered her.

But Maggie had been dead for ten years. He'd heard her dying screams, felt her burning arms around his neck.

He closed his eyes tightly. It was, of course, only another form of the dream. He was home in Meadowville. Mrs. Paige had said that Maggie would be coming back now that he was home. It was only a form of the dream, haunting him once again. Thus he explained it to himself.

He opened his eyes, stared at the foot of the yard. It was empty. The shadows still and unmoving. No one, nothing, was there.

He went to bed telling himself that he had imagined it. He felt closer to Maggie here than anywhere else. That was why he'd thought he'd seen her.

In the morning he called Richard to tell him that he was going to stay, and immediately started back to New York to get ready for the move.

CHAPTER 4

Liz slowly walked away from the Vickery house. She had stood in the shadows at the foot of the yard and stared up at the light in the second-floor bedroom window, planning what she would say to Claude. But in the end she hadn't been able to do it. Not knowing that he had had a glimpse of her, she started for home.

The idea had come to her when her mother had looked at her, lavender eyes childlike and shining, and said with absolute certainty, "Now Claude's back, I know Maggie will be too. I feel her so close. I *feel* her, Liz. I can almost hear her laughter. She'll come back because she loved Claude."

Liz didn't answer. Her mother would believe what she wanted to. Her mother wanted to believe that Maggie could return from the grave. Her mother believed that Maggie had loved Claude. But Maggie hadn't been what her mother thought, and the love her mother believed in had never existed.

Liz knew. She had listened to Maggie's midnight confidences. She had heard Maggie slip from the house to go with

Red, with Claude, and yes, even with Richard once. Maggie would never come back for Claude. And she had said, *There's something funny about all the Vickerys, I guess. Look at what Dane did. It shows up, doesn't it? And John's such a creep. Claude is too in a way. I just don't know about him any more. Too bad because it was fun for a while. He's so . . . intense, that Claude. But I can always go back to Red, I guess.*

Liz had never known for sure how much of what Maggie had said was fantasy, how much was truth. It didn't matter any more.

Except that Liz suddenly realized what she was thinking. If Maggie had loved Claude, then maybe she would come back. But since she hadn't . . .

That was when she'd told her mother she wanted to take a walk, and grabbed her coat and hurried to the Vickery house. She was going to tell him again that he must stay away from her mother, even say that it was bad for him too to be in Meadowville. But then she found she couldn't do it. The one time would have to be enough.

Angry with herself, she returned home. But as she closed the door she heard the whispering again.

Later, as a single lamp lit a corner of the room, Liz was helping her mother get ready for bed.

Ellen Paige swallowed her pills with a sip of water. "Did you have a nice walk?" she asked finally.

Liz said it had been pleasant.

"You should try to get out more. You need to do things. See people."

Liz didn't answer. Mrs. Baldwin was paid a standard sitter's fee, and it added up quickly.

"I never meant to be a bad mother," Ellen said. "Not to Maggie. Not to you. I never wanted to hurt you."

"Oh, mom! You haven't. Don't talk that way."

Ellen rubbed her slim hands, looked from them into Liz's face. "If it weren't for me, you and Richard would be married. You're right for each other, and belong together. Do you think I don't know? Do you think it doesn't matter to me?"

"Mom, please . . ."

"It does, Liz. I care deeply. More than you can imagine," Ellen went on. "But I can't change it. So *you* pay. You pay for my sins."

"Mom, no! There are no sins. You've been ill. It's not your fault. Don't you understand that? I'm here with you because I want to be. *Want* to be, mom." Liz believed it then. Her fears were forgotten momentarily. So were those fleeting moments, scarcely faced, when she wondered bitterly if she would ever be free to live her own life.

Ellen didn't answer.

Later Liz called Richard. "When is Claude leaving?" she demanded.

"I'll talk to you tomorrow," Richard told her.

"But why not now? What's going on?"

"I'll tell you all about it tomorrow," he said.

She said "good-bye," and put down the phone, frowning. Richard was being evasive. Something was wrong. Something to do with Claude Vickery.

Chapter 5

It was the day after John Vickery's funeral—a quiet Monday morning on Main Street.

Vernon Meese looked through the window of the Depot Cafe, watching a pickup truck head into an angle parking space. He tried to imagine the street crowded with cars, people hurrying into the shops. It was a nice thought. And it could happen. If nothing went wrong.

He intended to talk about that as soon as Willie Harker joined him in the booth known as the Executive Suite because it was always reserved for Vernon and a group of his friends.

Meanwhile he was thinking about the Vickerys and the Paiges. He had always had it in for them. Mostly because they'd been in Meadowville forever, and therefore had a head start on him. Not that the Paiges counted any more. After all, Morgan Paige was now long dead, and the two women weren't what a man would call competition.

Vernon had places to go. He didn't intend to let anyone stand in his way.

He'd come to town during the Second World War, a cook in the big Army camp that had been closed six months after the fighting ended in Europe. He'd married a town girl in the meantime. He went into her father's insurance business, and took it over when her father died.

But even after all these years he didn't feel he was accepted as he should be in Meadowville. Though he was chairman of the Council of Aldermen now, and had been on the board of the First Meadowville Farmers and Mechanics Bank for ten years, he still didn't feel that he was given his due. One day soon he planned to be the town mayor. One day there'd be a Meese Boulevard and a Meese Mall.

There was a smile on his round face when Willie Harker joined him.

The waitress brought Willie his coffee and refilled Vernon's cup. Then Willie said, "Sorry it took me so long. Red Stanton was giving me a hassle."

"A hassle?"

"He says a tire I sold him went bad too soon."

"Did it?"

"Maybe. Only if it did, then it wasn't the tire. It was him and how he treated it. You know Red."

Vernon did, and what he knew he didn't care for. There was something unpleasant about Red's grin, about the snake tattoo that almost seemed to crawl on his wrist.

Willie rubbed the bristles on his jaw. "I gave him back his money anyhow. Good public relations. Customer is always right. You know what I mean."

Vernon understood. Nobody wanted to get into it with Red. You never knew what the man would do. And he had some friends you'd just as soon not meet. A bunch of them that hung out in the Glass Slipper, a bar on the fringes of town. Not that Red himself had been in trouble. He hadn't. Not yet anyhow. It was just that you had a feeling he could be. Or that he could just blow up and start throwing around whatever he had in his hands.

"Speak of the devil," Willie said under his breath.

Red Stanton and two of his construction crew came in and took seats at the counter. The three wore dusty jeans, boots and tan shirts. Red flipped a salute at Willie, grinned at Vernon and turned his back.

Vernon decided he'd wait until Red and his boys left before talking business with Willie.

"It looked like everybody was at John Vickery's funeral yesterday," Willie said.

Vernon knew that meant Willie had the same thing on his mind that Vernon himself did. He shook his head slowly from side to side, and shot a glance at Red's broad back.

Willie understood. "But Claude's coming home . . . I couldn't figure that."

There were a lot of stories about the Vickerys and the Paiges. Vernon liked to tell them. One concerned how Meadowville got its name. It was said that the two families had always lived together in amiable competition until a meeting was called to choose a formal name for the town. What began as a reasonable discussion developed into a brawl with drawn knives. Before blood was shed, a John Vickery and a Bill Paige were pulled apart and talked into leaving the choice to a fresh deck of cards, with the man who drew the ace to do the naming. John Vickery drew the ace of spades. Bill Paige drew the ace of clubs. Amid hoots and hollers they deferred to the golden-haired dance hall girl who had moved in a month before. She picked the name Meadowville. That night both men proposed to her. She told them she'd give them her answer in the morning. But when morning came, she was gone. They never saw her again.

Vernon also liked to tell about the day that Dane Vickery brought the money back to the bank and gave it to the board of directors. And how Dane looked, and what he must have felt. And finally, how he'd walked out alone.

But his favorite one was about Maggie Paige, straitlaced Judge Morgan Paige's daughter, and how Vernon had seen Maggie making the two-backed beast with some kid he'd noticed hitching through town hardly an hour before. That was what he almost started to repeat to Willie now, but he stopped himself in time. After all, Maggie was dead, and so was her father, and poor old Ellen Paige was a cripple and a nut. So Vernon started to talk about the time Dane had brought the money back to the bank.

Willie said sourly, "Listen, I've heard that a dozen times before."

Vernon's face mimed silent disgust as he again looked at Red, who was getting to his feet. In a little while he and his crew had gone.

When the door slammed shut, Willie said, "You think Claude's coming back means anything?"

"I don't know. But it better not."

"I wonder if he's really okay now."

Vernon said grudgingly that he thought Claude was as okay now as he'd ever been. Which wasn't saying much.

"That's what I mean," Willie said. "And the nerve of him. Standing there, saying he's sorry to Mrs. Paige. As if that made any difference."

"He had to say something, I guess."

Willie thought that over. "He probably figured that was as good as anything," he said finally.

"I don't give a damn about Claude. It's what John Vickery's done that worries me."

"I've been wondering about that," Willie said. He didn't care at all about John Vickery. He'd never had much to do with the man, or with his family, and never had expected to. Once in a while he'd done Dane Vickery a favor, like giving Claude a summer job. But Dane had always paid him back.

But Willie Harker had grease under his nails from a lifetime of working with cars. He'd learned the mechanic's trade working for somebody else. He'd had little schooling, and didn't miss it. His wife was from St. Louis and thought that Meadowville was heaven and her Willie the best man there. He was satisfied to be who he was and what he was, but just now he had his eye on some big money. Which was why he was wondering what John Vickery had done. Willie and Vernon had cooked up a good deal between them. But John could have queered it. He owned a good-sized piece of property out on the highway. Vernon owned double that amount north of him. Willie owned nearly double that amount south. They had to get their hands on what was in between.

"It's why I wanted to see you. Computo-Sales."

Willie nodded. There was his big money. In the land Computo-Sales would buy. But only if he and Vernon could offer all three parcels.

"If John Vickery louses us up . . ." It was perfect. Just what the town needed. A clean industry that would bring in jobs, money. A push for land. A push for construction. More people. More money. Vernon looked out at Main Street and imagined

74

fleets of cars and trucks, herds of shoppers spilling off the vacant sidewalks.

"It won't be John that wrecks it," Willie was saying. "It'll be Claude. Else what the hell is he doing here?"

Vernon took a cigar from his vest pocket. He bit off its end, lit it with slow deliberation. Nothing was going to stop him. When he was mayor he'd get them to change the law, wipe out the Council of Aldermen. He'd run things his way. And from Meadowville he could maybe leapfrog to the state capital. Even to Washington. Who knew where it could end?

"Claude's not going to stay around long" he said positively. "You wait. One day. Two. And he'll be on his way."

A few minutes later Dr. Detrick passed by. He stopped to talk of the weather, then mentioned that he'd heard via the town grapevine that somebody had seen Claude Vickery driving out of town in his rented car.

Vernon and Willie grinned at each other.

"I guess it's okay," Vernon said.

"Sure," Willie agreed. "No need to worry about him. Just like you said."

CHAPTER 6

It was the same Monday morning. The doors to the office of the Registry of Wills opened ten minutes late by the electric clock.

Richard finished the cup of sour machine-made coffee and went in. He waited, tense, while the clerk completed what was obviously a personal phone call. Some three-quarters of an hour later, the documents had been filed for probate. He did a few other errands in the county seat, then headed back to Meadowville and his office.

A dark cloud had obscured the sun and from the distance there were growls of thunder. He felt relieved that he'd gotten things going. Claude was on his way back to New York, preparing for the move to town. Richard expected him to return within two weeks. So far it was all going as smoothly as Richard had hoped.

By mid-afternoon he realized that it wasn't going to be as simple as he had thought.

Vernon Meese called for an appointment. He told June

Stanton, Richard's secretary, that he wanted to see Richard on an urgent matter of business. He was bringing Willie Harker with him because Willie wanted to see Richard too.

June relayed the message between squeals of fright as thunder cracked through the room. She had hardly gone back to her desk when she appeared again, now accompanied by Liz.

"I have to talk to you, Richard. Right now," Liz said.

He waved June away, closed the door and pointed to a chair. Liz was pale, and there were dark circles under her eyes. He wished now that he'd explained to her what was going to happen when she called him the night before. He'd felt he shouldn't say anything until the will was filed. It had been a mistake. She'd already heard about it from somebody. It would have been better coming from him. He hitched a thigh on the edge of the desk and looked down at her. "What's the matter, Liz?"

"What's this about Claude? That's what I want to know. When I asked you last night . . ."

He grinned at her. "Our never-failing grapevine has done its job, hasn't it?"

"It's not funny, Richard."

"I know. I wanted to tell you myself. But the papers had to go in first."

"Then it's true. He's coming back to stay."

"Yes. He told me this morning before he left. He'll be back as soon as he makes the arrangements in New York."

"But it's . . . it's ridiculous. What's he going to do here? Why is he doing it?"

"Didn't the grapevine tell you about John's will?"

"Yes. Of course. But why's he doing it?" Her face was white. Her hands shook. "He can't stay here in Meadowville!"

"He has to. For two years. If he's going to inherit."

Liz shook her chestnut head back and forth violently.

"Now wait, Liz. You know Claude has the right to John's property. You wouldn't want to deny him that. No matter how you feel about him."

"It's not how I feel about him," she cried. "That doesn't matter. It's just that I'm . . . I'm worried." She folded her trembling hands in her lap. Her eyes were shiny with tears when she raised them to Richard's. "I'll bet you talked him into it. He'd have wanted to stay away. Just as he has for the past ten years. But you made him decide he wanted the money."

"I told him what was in the will, and what I just told you. About his rights, I mean."

"You always had a soft spot for him," she said accusingly.

"He did a lot for me, Liz."

She ignored that and went on. "And even after you knew what he'd done . . ."

"What he'd done," Richard said softly. "But all that he did was have an automobile accident. It could have happened to anyone."

"But it happened to him. And to Maggie."

Eyes quizzical, voice quiet, Richard said, "This isn't like you, Liz."

"Maybe you don't know the real me," she answered. "Maybe I'm not all sweetness and light and golden charity. Maybe I'm just a rotten old human being."

"Okay," he said, and grinned. "Maybe you're a vicious, narrow-minded, stubborn demon, disguised as my Liz. Just the same, I'd like to know what's really bothering you. It's not what happened ten years ago. I know that much. It's got something to do with now, hasn't it?"

She took a deep breath and looked at him silently for a moment. "Don't you see? It's my mother. I'm worried about what Claude's being here could do to her."

Richard was silent, waiting.

"It reminds her."

"She doesn't need reminding, Liz. She never forgets. So it won't make any difference."

"The thing is," she said slowly, "you don't really understand. That's what it is. You think you can just turn things off, like a spigot turns off water. Twist it as hard as you can, so there are no more leaks. But the past isn't water. And it's not like that. You can't turn it off hard. You can't stop the leaks. It creeps through, comes through. It never stops."

"That's not how it has to be. When something's done, it's done. If people are willing to have it that way."

"Willing? As if will has anything to do with it." She went on in a barely audible voice, "Richard, I'm . . . I'm scared."

She was trying now to be honest—with herself, and with him. Because it was the right way, the only way. But how to put it so he would know what she meant when even she wasn't sure? How would she tell him why she was so afraid?

He leaned over her, smoothed her hair, then cupped her cheeks in his big hands. "Liz, stop it. Your mother's going to be all right. She'll come out of it one of these days."

In words so soft that he could hardly hear them, she asked, "But what if mom is . . . is . . . not what we think? Suppose she knows something we don't? And somehow, someway . . ." With the words said, she wished them back. She knew what they sounded like. She could feel her heart pounding violently. God knew what he would think.

"Now, look," he said. "We don't even have to talk about that. We both know the answer."

His patient look, his careful voice, his certainty—all of it reminded her of how her father had spoken to her mother. *Ellen, it can't happen. No one rises from the grave. Not even our Maggie.* It reminded Liz of how she spoke to her mother now. *Oh, mom, don't. You know . . . you know . . .*

Silently, hopelessly, Liz swore to herself that she would never mention it to Richard again. Never. Never. No matter what happened. She would never again ask, *What if . . . ?*

Forcing a quick smile, she said aloud, "Listen to me, will you." Her laugh was almost a real one. "I'm beginning to sound like my mother." That frightened Liz too. She said hurriedly, "I don't mean that, either."

"You've still got your sense of humor, so I guess you're okay."

"Yes," she told him. "I'm okay. But if only you hadn't found Claude. Why did you have to look so hard?"

She knew why. It was because Richard was Richard. He felt that he owed Claude. He'd told her that. But there was more. Richard was loyal. To himself and to what he believed in. To his friends. And he was stubborn, especially when he thought he was right. And nobody could change his mind when he did. It was all part of why she loved him. She knew that. Still, she wished he hadn't looked so hard for Claude . . .

"I didn't have to. He wasn't hiding. I inquired, very superficially. And that was it. Just remember, please, Liz, that it was my job. And a moral obligation. I couldn't ignore the provisions of John's will. I couldn't pretend to make a search and let it

80

go." He paused. Claude had been his friend when he had needed one. He added, "And I didn't want to either."

Lightning exploded near the house, filling the room with blue light followed immediately by the sharp crackle of nearby thunder. When it was quiet again, she got up.

"I'll tell you what I think," she said. "You're going to wish you had sent John to another lawyer. You're going to wish you had nothing to do with it. The whole town knows what John's will said. I'll bet it took half an hour for the word to go around. And everybody knows as well as you and I do what John had in mind. Punishment. John wanted Claude to be here. To be here and to hurt. Maybe Claude doesn't know. Maybe he doesn't care. But John wanted him to suffer. You can be sure Meadowville will oblige. Someway or other, it'll make him wish he'd never come home."

With the thunder gone the room was quiet except for the sudden rattle of rain at the windows.

"I hope not, Liz," Richard said slowly.

"You'll see," she said, and left . . .

A few minutes later, June, pale faced and twisting her hands, told him that Willie Harker and Vernon Meese were waiting. He grinned at her. "Storm's over. And nothing happened."

"Lightning," she muttered. "Thunder."

"Nothing to be scared of."

"But I am."

He couldn't talk her out of being scared of storms any more than he could talk Liz out of being scared. He'd been wrong to try. He should have been more understanding. He decided he'd talk to her about it again that night. He went out to greet the waiting men and led them into his office.

When they were seated he asked what he could do for them.

Vernon Meese's thin blond wings of hair were wet, plastered to his head with rain. He spoke with a cigar clenched in his teeth. "You can tell us just what provisions John Vickery wrote into that will of his that everybody's talking about. This morning I heard that Claude's left town. And good riddance to him. Maybe a couple of hours later I hear that he's coming back so he can get everything John left. I want to know what's going on. So does Willie here. And so does the Council of Aldermen. Although we're just visiting you unofficially for now."

"It's all a matter of public record," Richard said.

"You can say that again. It's so public everybody in town is talking about it." Willie Harker shifted in his chair. "We want to know if what they're saying is true. One thing. Is Claude really coming back?"

"Yes, Willie. And I guess the rest of it you heard is true too."

"You mean all that crazy stuff is right?" Willie was seeing the Computo-Sales deal fall through, and the big money he had counted on as his flying away. "If Claude stays here for two years, he gets John's property? If he doesn't, then the town gets it?"

If the town got it, Willie thought, then he was okay. Vernon would make sure the town sold the acreage between his lot and Willie's to Computo-Sales. And Willie would have what he'd worked for all his life. Security. His gas station and the used-car lot next to it did okay. But with prices yo-yoing and parts harder to get, they were uncertain. He wanted security. For his wife. For him. No boats, no fancy cars, no new house for Willie Harker. Just enough money in the bank so when he got older and needed it, it would be there waiting for him.

"You've got it right," Richard was saying. "That's how John Vickery wanted it. And that's what I wrote in his will."

"It sounds funny to me," Vernon told him.

Richard leaned back in his chair. The sun had come out after the storm. A single ray glowed in a bar of light across the papers on his desk. "It's as straightforward as it could be."

"But Claude pulled up stakes years ago," Willie complained.

"Had them pulled up for him, is what you mean." Vernon went on, "And they should have stayed that way. Nobody in this town wants him back." He puffed on his cigar. "How come he found out that John had died?"

"I called and told him."

"You always were pretty buddy-buddy with him, weren't you?" Willie said disgustedly.

Richard wasn't surprised. He'd known that was coming. "Claude was a friend of mine. Yes. If that's what you mean." He paused, then said deliberately, "And he's still a friend of mine for that matter. But that's got nothing to do with it. He's got his rights."

"So have we," Willie said. He turned to Vernon. "I guess we got to talk about this some."

But Vernon remained in his seat. He was thinking about the situation. He, like Willie, was going to lose a lot that he'd counted on. But even worse, he saw his dream of a Meese Mall drifting away. "Any way to break that will?" he asked.

"No. I was careful when I wrote it. But what would you want to do that for?"

"The Council of Aldermen is going to ask me. That's the first thing it's going to want to know. Because of the property John Vickery left."

"To Claude first. The town second," Richard said quietly.

"Listen, whose side are you on?" Willie was heated now. He leaned forward. "We don't owe Claude anything. We owe this town everything. Everything we can do for it. Why, that house, the land around it." Inspired, he rushed on. "Can you imagine what it would be for a recreation center?"

Vernon looked surprised. He hadn't thought of that before, but he began to think of it now. "Yes, just think about that, Richard. A recreation center for the kids. It's just what we need. And the property out of town . . . it could be income producing in no time at all. Meadowville's going to be a ghost town in not too many years if we don't do something about it. This here, from John, it could turn the whole thing around." Then, more quietly, waving his cigar at Willie, "Of course Willie and me, we're jumping the gun. We oughtn't to be counting on what we don't have." Vernon turned back to Richard, "I guess we'd better talk this over a little."

"I think we've covered it pretty well."

Vernon ignored that. "What do you know about Claude?" he asked.

"Just about what you know, I imagine."

"He's been living in New York. Right?" The way Vernon said "New York" it was plain he didn't think much of it.

But Richard nodded. He didn't yet see where this was going. It might be a good idea to find out.

"Working at drawing comic strips. Right?"

"Yes. I've seen them too. Maybe you have. In the Sunday papers from St. Louis. They're signed 'Vick.'"

"I don't read the damn things," Willie said. "Can he make a living at that?"

"A very good living."

"Then why'd he jump at coming back where nobody wants him?"

84

"In the first place, he didn't exactly jump. In the second . . ."

Vernon cut in. "You had to talk him into it?"

Richard didn't answer, but said instead, "Regardless of anything else, there's the inheritance. You ought to be able to see why he'd be interested in that. Since you're so interested in it yourself."

"For the town," Willie told him. "It's just part of Vernon's job. Being on the council, the head of it."

Vernon spent a little more time probing. He asked how long Claude had been out of the insane asylum, and if Richard believed that he was really cured of what had ailed him, and if Richard thought that anybody ever really got cured of being crazy. Willie put in that he thought Claude had acted funny at the funeral, but of course that was only his opinion, though a lot of other people had thought so, too. Vernon asked if Claude was married, or had been. And whether Richard had seen him before John died and whether John himself had.

Richard began to see where the questions were going. Vernon was trying to get something on Claude that Vernon could use. It made Richard angry, and he got testy. "Look, it's got nothing to do with you," he said finally. "It won't until Claude decides he doesn't want to live in Meadowville for two years."

"I guess that's about right," Vernon agreed. He got to his feet. "I don't mind saying I'm surprised at you. You ought to have realized what you were doing to the town. And to yourself, too."

Vernon was referring to the fact that Richard did the legal work for the Council of Aldermen.

"I had no choice, Vernon." Richard didn't like the sound

of that. It was too apologetic. He added, "And even if I'd had a choice, I'd have done it the same way."

"You could have chosen not to find Claude, couldn't you?" Willie asked.

"Not and stayed honest, I couldn't."

"Oh, yeah," Willie said thoughtfully. "I see."

When the two men had gone, Richard let his shoulders sag. He leaned on his desk, considering. If he hadn't found Claude it would have been all right. No one would have been the wiser. No one would have cared. The trouble was that *he* would have known, and he would have cared. Claude was due what he was due. If he could earn it. And it was beginning to look as if he'd have to.

Outside on the street Willie squinted at Vernon. "That was a damn fool thing Richard Braun did. Once an outsider, always an outsider."

Vernon didn't like that. He'd been an outsider himself once. He didn't like to be reminded of it. On the other hand, if Willie had recalled when Vernon came to town he wouldn't have said that. When Vernon was in the car, with Willie beside him, he said, "It's because Richard was friends with Claude, Willie."

"Well, he's not the only lawyer in town."

"Don't be hasty."

"I'm not hasty. I'm sensible. One hand washes the other. You scratch my back and I'll scratch yours. That's what makes the world go round. How come Richard Braun thinks he's different?"

"I guess he didn't think about that."

"It's going to kill us with Computo-Sales," Willie said.

"Maybe not." But Vernon thought it probably would. Unless he could do something about it.

"Listen, they're not going to wait for this to get untangled. And you know what it means to us. That property out of town's right in the middle. Between your land and mine. They need all of it, or none of it."

"Maybe," Vernon repeated. "And if so, Meadowville's the loser. More than you and I lose, Willie. The town needs this. A nice clean industry. All those people coming in. New houses to be built. The stores full. When I think of it . . ."

Willie laughed harshly. "Yeah, when you think of it . . . and when I do . . ."

In a little while they were back where they had been that morning. The Depot Cafe was emptier now than it had been earlier. The only other customers were Red Stanton and one of his crew. They had their heads together, whispering like conspirators.

Vernon watched them as he drank his coffee, wondering what they were up to. Probably no good. That was what first put it in his mind.

"One thing. You'd better take a run up to Chicago. See how much time we actually have," Willie said.

Vernon nodded. "I wonder what Claude's really figuring on doing here."

"Maybe he won't stick it out."

"Richard will be advising and pampering him."

But Vernon was thoughtful. He didn't like the idea of having anything to do with Red. On the other hand, Red could have his uses. Vernon stood up. "I'm going to ask Red Stanton to come over."

Red came back with Vernon and slid into the booth, grinning at Willie. "I never thought I'd be sitting here." He twisted to look out the big window. There were a few cars moving on Main Street. The puddles left by the rain were nearly dry. "I sure do like your view."

"I guess you've heard the news," Vernon said.

"Yeah. First I heard Claude left for good. Then I heard he's coming back for two years so he can get John's money. And that screws the town."

"And how it screws the town," Willie agreed.

At this moment the unspoken conspiracy was born. If it had been anybody but a Vickery involved, nothing would have happened. The past would have been forgotten, the loss to the town shrugged off. But the Vickerys had been too well known, too successful, and had been so for too long. Claude stood for all of them now.

Vernon looked Red in the eye. "The town gets screwed more than you know. The council figured to make the Vickery house a recreation center for the kids. We can forget it, I guess." Vernon knew he'd made a direct hit when he saw Red's expression. The gouges and scars turned beet red. As his brows drew down, he looked dangerous to Vernon.

That was a funny thing about Red. It just didn't make sense. But he was crazy about kids. The only thing that would take him away from drinking beer at the Glass Slipper on his time off was to come to the council meeting to agitate for street-crossing guards or more sports equipment funds or money for special out-of-town sightseeing trips. If Red had another interest, aside from making trouble, Vernon didn't know what it was. Seeing the man's scowl, he hoped he hadn't made a mistake.

"You mean Claude's wrecking a center for the kids?" Red said.

"If we don't get the house, how can we do it?"

For the next hour Vernon and Willie talked about what the town would have done if Claude hadn't come back. They didn't mention Computo-Sales. They didn't say Claude should be run out of town on a rail. They just discussed what the town had lost. Recreation center, public swimming pool. They just wondered aloud if Claude was still dangerous.

Red didn't say much. But he was listening.

He dropped his lunch pail on the table and glared at June. "Are you planning to get dinner for me? Or are you just going to sit there and stare at the wall?"

"My feet hurt, Red. I've been running around ever since I got out of bed this morning."

"I'm sorry for you. Sitting at a desk all day . . . banging on a typewriter . . . What do you do, answer the phone with your feet, and type with them too?"

"He had a lot of people coming in. One thing after another. It just wouldn't stop. And he didn't like it either. I could tell. And then there was the storm."

"He. He. He. You mean Richard Braun?" The name didn't taste good on Red's lips. He wanted to spit it out. Damn Richard Braun. It was his fault that Claude was back in Meadowville, ready to grab what really belonged to the town. What Vernon Meese and Willie Harker hadn't known was that he was also stirring up old memories for Red. Memories that bothered him.

June was giving him a look of injured innocence. "Of course I mean Richard Braun. He's my boss, isn't he?" She waited for acknowledgment, received none and finally went on. "What's it all about anyhow. Vernon Meese and Willie Harker came in and went away mad."

Red chuckled. "So I heard."

"You heard? About that?" Her eyes widened. "What's it got to do with you?"

"Nothing. And if you weren't so dumb you'd have told me about it a long time ago."

"Told you what?" Her bewilderment was in her voice now. "I wish I knew what you're talking about."

"About John Vickery. His will. Only a lamebrain like you wouldn't have known it was important."

"What about him and his will?"

Red explained, spacing the words slowly and carefully.

"Oh," she said. "I see now. Only I never knew anything about that."

"You didn't know about the will?"

She shook her head. "I remember when John Vickery, that old sourpuss, came in. I guess it was maybe a year ago. Just after I started working for Richard. But there was never any more about it."

"Then who typed up the will, or whatever you have to do?"

"Whoever it was, it wasn't me."

"So he was keeping it a secret?"

"Who was?"

"Your boss, stupid."

She pursed her lips. "I don't like it when you call me that, Red."

He laughed. But he was thinking about Richard doing his own typing so June couldn't put anything on the grapevine. Richard hadn't wanted anybody to know what was going to happen. Not until the last minute. Not until it was too late to do anything about it. Only was it too late? Red wondered.

"And I'll tell you something else," June said. "I never saw Claude Vickery except at the funeral yesterday and don't know him from Adam. But I feel sorry for him. The way everybody's acting . . . you'd think he had a bad case of something awful. Staring at him and whispering behind their hands. And now, you."

"You don't know what you're talking about, stupid. As usual."

"What about him then?"

"You've already heard about it."

"All I heard was he had an accident. That girl got killed. He had a nervous breakdown. It's over. Does he have to pay for it forever?"

"He hasn't paid anything. Yet," Red said. "Only a lame-brain like you would think he had."

She uncurled, rose. "I still feel sorry for him. I'd feel sorry for anybody who managed to get away from this town and then had to come back."

"You can get out anytime you want to. Nobody's stopping you."

"I know." She paused at the kitchen door. "Only I don't know where to go."

He caught up the lunch pail, slung it at her as hard as he could. It bounced off the door frame, leaving a long white scar in the woodwork. "One of these days . . ."

But she had gone. He heard pots and pans banging in the sink. One of these days, he told himself, he'd throw her out. And that would be that. He should have done it a long time ago. He hadn't, though he wasn't sure why. Except that he didn't have anybody else. And he damn well knew it wasn't good to be alone . . . .

He'd never had anybody. That was the thing. Not since that brief time with Maggie. And he'd lost her too. To Claude Vickery first. And then to her grave.

He'd known all the time he couldn't keep her. What did Maggie Paige want with a nobody like him? He told himself to quit lying. Yeah. Okay. There'd been those few weeks when he maybe kidded himself. And hated himself for it too. Knowing she'd only wanted to satisfy her curiosity about him. About the nobody, the roughest kid in town. And then dropped him. For Claude. And it only proved what he'd always known. He wasn't good enough for the Paiges.

He had been the son of the town barber. Red was the shoeshine boy for longer than he wanted to remember. Red's mother had been long gone even then. When his father walked into the side of a truck after a prolonged drunken weekend, Red was alone, and the funeral had to be on the house.

He managed to finish high school by being handyman and gardener for the Paiges and the Vickerys and their like. Summers he worked with a building crew. He was lucky to have learned a trade. When the others went to college he was drafted. He spent eighteen months in Viet Nam. He had a bad war and came home scarred. He put in a few years drifting around the country. He let his hair grow long. He wore love beads. He went from the dead Haight-Ashbury to the mountains of Taos to a commune in Pennsylvania. Along the way he picked up June.

In another time she would have been called simple. At least by people who didn't know where she'd been and what she'd done. Those who knew would say she'd been permanently affected by angel dust. Sometimes she knew who she was and where she lived. Sometimes she floated. She could take directions, do her job, be on time, type and answer the phone. She remembered to bathe, comb her hair, even to cook a meal. But there was always a part of her drifting on invisible currents. She was like a shell without a kernel . . . .

He heard her yelling now. "Soup's on. If you want it."

He went into the kitchen. He kept his eyes away from the stack of dishes in the sink as he tasted the soup. Tomato. Not very hot. He ate, not waiting for her to join him.

When he had emptied the bowl, he looked up at her. "You keep your ears and eyes open. I want to know what Claude Vickery does. And what Richard does."

"Are you back on that?"

His face got tight, and he gave her a level look. "I'm not kidding, June. I want to know. You hear me?"

"Okay, okay." She yawned, stretched. "If I remember. God, my feet hurt."

That night Liz woke up suddenly. She lay still for a moment, listening. What had she heard? Could it have been footsteps? She rose quickly, hurried to look in at her mother. Ellen Paige didn't stir. Her room was still.

Shivering, Liz went back to bed. For a long time she lay awake, staring into the shadows, and remembering Maggie.

CHAPTER 7

Three weeks later a half-empty Continental Trailways bus
labored under the red and gold maples on Main Street. It
blasted its horn at a green Volare with dealer's tags that was
slowing for a turn into Willie Harker's used-car lot. Then, with
much complaining of brakes, it made a hard left into the bus
depot.

Meadowville had once had a railroad that made scheduled
stops there twice daily, but that was long gone. It had once had
an interstate highway that fed into Century Boulevard, but a
bypass put in twelve years before had broken that lifeline. A
small landing field, unused since the Army moved out, had
once serviced a few small planes. It had since gone to weed.

The depot was Meadowville's point of entry for the traveler
without an automobile. But it wasn't busy. Its platform was
empty. Two men chatted in its clean waiting room. A clerk
seemed to be dozing behind the stand that sold newspapers,
notions and candy. There were, however, a few people in the

Depot Cafe, and Vernon Meese was holding the fort in the Executive Suite.

Sunlight and a fresh October breeze streamed through the wide-open doors of the cafe and through the depot waiting room.

A single passenger got off the bus to stretch her legs during the fifteen-minute stop. She noticed the quietness of Main Street, the sunlight, the autumn breeze, but wasn't aware of anything else that could have led her to make her sudden decision.

She would stop for a while. She went back to the bus, found the driver. Within a few minutes she had her two suitcases, had hired the only cab waiting and was on her way to the Meadow-ville Hilton.

When she checked in she signed the register Dina Forrest.

She was smallish, with long blond hair that she sometimes rolled up into a bun. Now it hung down her back, very straight and clean. She had a slender figure, though her plain linen suit didn't show off the curves it covered. Her hands were tiny, square, the nails cut short and unpolished.

She unpacked her clothes, took a shower and climbed into bed to watch television.

It felt good to stretch out on fresh, starched sheets. Maybe that was why she'd decided not to get back on the bus for a while. Just so she could feel the starched sheets on her skin.

She'd started the trip in New York. Her destination was San Francisco. But she was in no hurry, had left nothing that mattered to her behind. She wasn't going to anything special ahead.

Rootless, free—that's what she was. She thought she was

lucky. Footloose. It meant not being tied down. That's what she was too.

She was close to thirty, although she looked a little younger than that. She was on her own. Another piece of luck. She'd worked steadily since she graduated from high school. She could hardly remember the different jobs she'd had. But she had saved seven hundred dollars. Now they were traveler's checks in her purse. She had some simple clothes. A few pairs of shoes. That was it. She owed nothing, and there was no one in debt to her.

She was looking for something, she supposed, though she didn't know what. And she didn't care. If she were destined to find it, she would, she thought—if not, so be it.

Meanwhile it felt good to rest in the hotel room. She'd stay a few days. Look around. Then she'd go on.

CHAPTER 8

Claude wore a long-sleeved blue shirt, a blue and white knit vest and a heavy blue corduroy jacket. It was a lot of clothes for noon on a sunny fall day, but he felt cold. He was impatient, too. He wanted to be settled in, to get to work, to start living. And everything took time. It was three weeks since John's funeral. The moving had taken longer than he had expected. He'd only been back five days.

He shuffled his feet and looked out of the window at the red and gold pumps in the service station. He remembered when they had been blue and white.

Willie continued the usual sales pitch. It wouldn't do him any good. Claude didn't like the way the transmission worked on the bronze Chevy. Nothing would change his mind.

"One owner, an old lady," Willie said. "She only drove it once or twice a week. To church. To do her shopping. Stuff like that."

Claude grinned.

Willie shrugged, led Claude out to look at a Volare. It was

four years old, green, only slightly scarred. Claude decided to give it a test drive. As he pulled into Main Street a Continental Trailways bus sailed by, blaring its horn at him.

He drove slowly, not thinking about where he was going. It startled him to find himself suddenly at the top of Dead Man's Bluff. He pulled over and lit a cigarette. The sun glinted on the church spire in the valley below. He thought of Maggie . . . Her arms around his neck, burning into his flesh . . . He had long since understood his sense of guilt, working it through with the therapists. He had tried to drag her from the burning wreck, but couldn't. And he knew also that if he hadn't freed himself he'd have died with her. He'd been driven to abandon her by the natural drive to save himself that all men have. There was no guilt. There was only love, and longing, and the hope that here, here where it had happened, he would feel close to her again.

He was sweating when he pulled into the used-car lot again. He told Willie he would take the car, waited while the papers were prepared. He signed them and, with dealer's tags in place, he went home.

Red Stanton and his crew had left their pickups in the driveway. Claude parked at the curb and got out.

There was the sound of an electric saw, pounding hammers and raised shouting voices. But, in spite of this, the street seemed peculiarly silent. It was as if everything had been muted. Claude let his breath out slowly. He had the feeling that he was waiting for something to happen, but he didn't know what it was.

There wasn't much for him to do. His books and records and work materials had arrived almost the same time he did. They were all properly put away. His clothing was neatly arranged in closets and drawers. When the remodeling of what had once been his father's library was completed, Claude would be ready to start work again.

It had surprised him that Red Stanton had turned up, asking to be given the job. Claude had asked Richard to recommend someone, and Richard had given him a couple of names. Claude had decided to get estimates from them, but that same night Red came by and Claude, looking into the slanted smile, had somehow been unable to send him away. Over a beer, they'd settled on plans and price.

The next day Red had started to move materials in. He assured Claude it would take no more than a week to install the big window and to redo the wiring for the two large fluorescent lamps Claude wanted.

When he stepped inside, the sound of the saw stopped, and he heard Red's deep voice. ". . . think it's a funny thing all right. A guy's been away ten years. He comes back, sees all his old friends. So what does he do? Nothing."

Listening, Claude was not surprised that Red was talking about him. It was to be expected. Claude knew he ought to have had the guts to tell Red somebody else was doing the job.

Even as he was thinking that, Claude wondered what he was supposed to have done. He'd said hello, spoken of the past. He'd said what he planned to do, when asked. He didn't know of anything else.

Without stopping he went upstairs, making sure he was noisy so that Red and the other men would know he was at home.

He paced the floor for an hour, trying to concentrate on the strip and on how it would go when he started to work. Nothing came to him. Finally he gave up.

He drove out to the Century Mall and bought a case of beer. Only Red was still there when he returned home. He gave Red a beer, which he drank quickly. Claude gave him another. They talked about the Iraqi attack on Iran. Red hoped the Iranians got smeared. They talked about the coming election. Red was for Ed Clark, but he wasn't going to vote. What was the point? he asked. After a third beer Red said he had to leave. He needed some things. He'd see Claude in the morning.

Claude hoped that the conversation would make a difference, would perhaps relieve some of the stiffness between him and Red. He didn't fool himself that they'd ever really been friends in the past. Not the way Claude and Richard had been. But they'd known each other when they were kids. Something of that ought to be left . . .

That night Red said to June, "He's trying to butter me up. Beer and politics won't do it though."

"Who?" she asked.

"Who? Who the hell do you think? Claude. That's who. And I want to know what's going on. Has he been in to talk to Richard?"

She shrugged.

"Listen, stupid. I told you to keep your ears and eyes open."

"I told you about the remodeling job, didn't I?"

"You keep listening. That's all," he said sourly. He was thinking about John Vickery's will . . .

And that night Claude had drinks and dinner with Richard. Richard had asked, "How are you managing? Is it okay?"

"Sure. It's going to be fine," Claude had said.

But he still had the feeling that something was going to happen. He was braced, expectant, though he didn't know for what.

The next morning, while he ate his breakfast, he could hear Red talking again.

"I tell you, if we keep up, we're going to be at war. Another Viet Nam. And that's okay for them as can figure a way not to go."

"And how's that?" one of the carpenters asked.

Red chuckled. "Last time, if you were in college you were okay." He paused, laughed once more. It wasn't a happy sound. "Or if you were in the funny farm, then that was okay too. As a matter of fact, being in the funny farm can be a damn good thing. Get you out of the Army. And if you're smart, keep you out of jail, too."

Claude lowered his cup to the table. Jail. Hard, hating voices. Judge Paige's whispered accusations. The funny farm . . . one-way glass and white camisoles . . . His shaking hands splashed hot coffee on the table, but he ignored it. What was Red trying to do? He must know Claude could hear every word he said. Or was he just not thinking?

Claude knew he should go in, tell Red to get the hell out and stay out. But it was easier to think about than to do. It was, the more Claude thought of it, impossible.

He didn't listen any more. He didn't want to know the rest of what Red might be saying. All he wanted was for Red to be gone. Only it would have to wait until the work was done.

Claude left his breakfast, got a jacket. Red's chuckle followed him outside.

As Claude was getting into the Volare, Willie Harker drove up. He waved.

Claude waited while Willie parked in front of him, then came over.

"See you're getting all fixed up," Willie said.

101

"I had to have a room to work in. With good light. A drawing board." Claude was wondering what brought Willie to see him but didn't want to ask.

Willie turned to look at the Vickery house. "I hate to see it changed," he said heavily. "Whenever I pass by, I think of John. Of your father."

Claude said nothing. It surprised him that Willie thought of them. He didn't remember that Willie had had any closeness to either of them years before.

"So you're really planning to stay on," Will said. He turned a questioning look on Claude. "I never figured you would. I thought when you left after the funeral you'd think it over and decide not to come back."

So that was what it was about. Claude kept his face expressionless, shoved his glasses higher on his nose. "Is that right, Willie?"

"It's what made sense to me. I mean, if I was in your shoes . . . after what happened . . . The memories would bother *me*. Of course, everybody's different. And they react different. I understand that."

Claude nodded uncertainly.

Willie went on. "I was driving past and saw you so I figured I'd stop. I was wondering about John's property. What you're going to do about it."

"I haven't thought about it yet."

"You better start thinking about it."

"It isn't mine, Willie. There's plenty of time."

"Yeah. I guess that's so." Willie sighed. "I never figured John would end up giving us such a hard time. Six months is one thing. Two years is another."

"I doubt John intended to make trouble for you," Claude

said dryly. He didn't ask what Willie was talking about. He didn't want to know about the hard time John was inflicting on anybody through his will, and didn't want to prolong the conversation either. He spoke quickly. "There's a couple of things on the Volare . . ."

"Bring her in," Willie told him, and paused. "You ought to think about what's going on. You're a Vickery. You've got responsibilities to Meadowville. If you hadn't turned up, we'd have had that house over there in just six months. And all the property John owned too."

"I didn't just 'turn up,'" Claude answered. "Richard called me."

"Sure. He had to. Once he found you." Willie didn't pretend enthusiasm. "Still, you ought to think about it. Maybe you owe the town something. Maybe you ought to give us a hunk of that property."

Claude said nothing. But he was asking himself, *What do I owe the town? What's he talking about? . . .*

They—the town—had deprived him of everything. A good opinion. Youth. Maggie. They weren't going to deprive him of all that was still left of what had been rightfully his.

"When you can," Willie was saying. "I mean after it's yours. And there's even a better way, you know. You could just pick up and leave."

So that was why Willie had just happened to come by. To suggest he leave town. Claude finally knew what he'd been expecting to happen, what he'd been waiting for, and now that he understood, he felt better.

"Why should I do that?" he asked quietly.

"I just told you. You owe us. But you always were a hard head. I remember how it was with you and your father and

John. Nothing they ever said was right, was it? Nothing they asked of you, wanted of you. You always had to have it your own way."

"Maybe you're right, Willie. But it seemed just the other way around to me."

When Willie had gone, Claude drove down to the used-car lot. There were small things, the windshield wiper that didn't work, a rattle in the door latch.

Willie was there, but Claude didn't talk to him. He waited while the mechanic checked the car over, and said he'd take care of it. Claude said he'd hang around.

Soon Willie joined him. "You want to take good care of that car. It's a good one, like I told you. And after what happened to you before, you'd better stay away from Dead Man's Bluff."

Claude didn't answer. He went across Main Street to the Depot Cafe and drank three cups of black coffee, waiting until the Volare was ready.

Later, Willie told Vernon about it. "I never saw a man so upset in my life. He didn't say a word. Just turned around and walked out. You'd have thought he had a guilty conscience or something. And I never meant a thing. I was just talking, of course."

Vernon nodded, chewing his cigar.

"He's crazy. He was crazy as a kid. I know. He worked for me, didn't he? That last summer. That's why they locked him up. And he never got over it. No matter what they say."

Willie went on to recount his conversation with Claude earlier that day. "I know you said I shouldn't bother to talk with him. It wouldn't do any good. But I figured I'd try. Only you were right. That boy didn't want to hear me."

At home that evening Claude thought about the day and

decided everybody in Meadowville was crazy, just as always. The town still hadn't gotten over what had happened. It still remembered Maggie's death. Still remembered that he'd been driving the car when she died. And still pretended that it had suffered a loss. But she'd been nothing to Willie Harker, to Red Stanton, to Vernon Meese. She'd been nothing to them.

Maggie's death was *his* loss. Claude's own. And his alone.

Towards dawn he saw the headlights cut through the shadows on Dead Man's Bluff. He felt the car jolt, heard the tires squeal, heard Maggie's screams. When he awakened he still felt her flaming arms around his neck.

He got out of bed, sweaty and shaking, damning the dream.

He was under control by the time Red and his crew came in. But he still felt frightened. He still felt as if he were waiting for something without knowing what it was. Except that he knew it had to be more than a visit from Willie.

Later he went downstairs.

"I can see it so plainly." Red was saying. "You close in the verandah. Give it a thick layer of insulation. And you end up with room for ping pong tables, see. Take out that wall there. And you have a billiard room. The kitchen's okay for setting up coffee and Cokes."

It was fantasy, and Red knew it. But he couldn't stop thinking about it. It had been in his head ever since Vernon Meese had told him what the Council of Aldermen would do if it got its hands on the Vickery house. The thing was, Red was a man who really liked kids. He saw himself in them, and he wanted to do something for them, something that really mattered.

But Claude, hearing Red's spoken-aloud daydream, said dryly, "I wasn't planning on changes like that, Red."

"Not for you," Red answered. "I was telling the boys what

a good rec hall this house could be. A real community center. We need something like that in Meadowville."

Claude shrugged and went out.

Walking, remembering the nightmare, he told himself that it was just like with Willie Harker. Red and Willie both wanted John's property for themselves. That's what it was. That, and nothing else. And they weren't going to get it. It was Claude's. And he was home for good. They weren't going to drive him away.

But he still shivered inside his clothes. Coming back wasn't the way he'd thought it would be.

When he finally paid attention to where he was, he saw that he was passing in front of the Paige house. He stopped abruptly, looking at the curtained windows. There was no movement there, no sound. The windows stared back at him like dead eyes.

He wanted to go in, badly. He could feel an urge pulsing like a tide inside him. He wanted to talk to Ellen Paige. About Maggie.

But what would she say? And what about Liz? After a moment, he forced himself to walk away.

It was Sunday morning. Vernon Meese watched his wife finish putting on her makeup. If she didn't hurry, they'd be late. As she took her furs from the closet, he thought it was too warm still for mink, but didn't say anything. He knew she liked to wear them and he himself liked for her to wear them. They underscored his success.

And he was only at the beginning. He felt like a juggler who had started five oranges in the air. Now he just had to keep them going. And there was no hurry. He had plenty of time for the momentum to develop and build. Plenty of time for the town to figure out how Claude Vickery was depriving it of what it was entitled to.

He was smiling when they started out for church.

CHAPTER 9

Liz held her breath and listened for a moment. No. No, there was no whispering now. So maybe it was okay finally. Maybe it was over for a while. She was smiling when she went into her mother's room.

Ellen Paige sat in her wheelchair near the window. She wore a green sweater over a white blouse and a strand of pearls was at her throat. A beige blanket was tucked around her knees.

"I was just going to call you, Liz," she said. "I was sitting here, thinking. About Claude."

"What about him, mom?" The casual question belied the sudden sinking in Liz's heart. Damn Claude. Liz didn't want to think of him. She didn't want her mother to think of him. As far as she was concerned, she'd as soon pretend that Claude didn't exist.

"It must be hard on him," Ellen said. "Being so alone, I mean. We know what that's like. I think we should invite him to dinner." She went on in a rush. "I thought he'd come by to see us. But maybe he's waiting to be asked. Maybe he's still as shy as he used to be."

Liz didn't tell her mother that she had told Claude to stay away. "He's been busy. He's having the house fixed up." There was bitterness in Liz's voice. Fixing a studio only showed that Claude intended to stay in Meadowville. She'd hoped, still hoped, he'd end up changing his mind. But it wasn't going to happen.

"Richard has seen him?" Ellen asked.

"Of course." Liz tried to sound noncommittal. But it bothered her that Richard had seen Claude since his return. She told herself that Richard was a grown man, could do what he wanted. But she wished he didn't want to spend time with Claude. It was like taking sides. Richard, with Claude. Against her. Against the town.

"I'm glad Claude is staying," Ellen told her, sudden light glowing in her faded eyes. "It'll be so much easier with him here."

"Mom!"

"Do you think I'm going to forget about inviting Claude if you delay long enough?"

"I'm not trying to make you forget about it. I just don't think it's time yet."

"I do." She added softly, "Liz, I won't forget."

"I have no hope of that, mom."

"No hope," Ellen agreed. The words were a long-drawn-out sigh around which her pale lips quivered. "How could I ever forget Maggie?"

"We're talking about Claude," Liz said. Her tone was sharp. She felt a chill between her shoulders. This was too much like listening to the whispers. "Claude," she repeated. But, of course, she knew how wrong she was. When her mother spoke of Claude she could only be thinking of Maggie. The two names were forever linked in her mind. A single breath. A single thought. And a single wish.

"It's fated," Ellen said breathlessly. "I know. I feel it. I've been waiting all this time. And now that Claude's come home . . ." The words died on a quick dry cough.

Liz rose swiftly. She took a small pill from a bottle on the table. "Under your tongue, mom."

Her mother shook her head from side to side, whispered, coughing still, "No, no. It's all right. No, Liz."

"Please."

Ellen sighed, accepted the pill. She slipped it under her tongue.

"You oughtn't to think of Claude so much," Liz told her.

"Poor Liz. You're afraid, aren't you?"

"Afraid of what? That you'll really bring Maggie back? Afraid that somehow Claude's being here will make the difference?" Liz's voice was quick and confident, giving no hint of the strange, frantic currents of her feelings. She went on, "No, mom. It's not that. I worry about what you're doing to yourself."

"It will happen."

"Mom, please. Never mind for now."

"It will. One day you'll see with your own eyes. You'll hear with your own ears. You'll follow me across the bridge between life and death."

Liz turned away abruptly. She couldn't bear any more. Her mother's eyes were suddenly bright with hope. Her voice was steady, though more breathless than it should have been. There was a believing smile on her blue lips. She looked perfectly all right. But she sounded mad. She *was* mad. How else to explain this? "Let's not talk about it any more," Liz said.

"I think about it, even when I'm not talking about it."

"I know," Liz said, and left the room.

In the kitchen, she busied herself at the sink, trying to clear her mind, trying to keep from throwing things. She knew she could never talk her mother out of the delusion, could never stop the pitiful whispering. Yet, once in a while, when it was no longer possible to control her tongue, Liz would hear herself trying. It was like blowing against a hurricane. The words were spun away, unheard.

A few minutes later, the wheelchair squeaked behind her. She turned.

"Liz, please don't be upset with me," Ellen said.

"I'm not."

"You act as if you are. Whenever I try to talk to you about Maggie, you argue or else you don't really listen."

"I'm sorry. I don't mean to cut you off. It's just that I'm worried that you strain yourself too much."

"If you're not upset with me, then telephone Claude. Or would you rather I do that?"

"You do. If you like," Liz said. "But don't be disappointed if Claude says he's too busy to come right now and puts you off." It was what Liz hoped would happen. She didn't want to see him in the Paige house. It would remind her too much of the way it used to be . . . Claude, waiting for Maggie at the foot of the steps. His sudden grin, that bright youthful look that seemed always to change his face completely. And Maggie, hugging a ragged brown teddy bear in her arms, saying, *He's deep, Liz. There's more to Claude than anybody sees. His feelings . . . oh, sometimes, he just plain scares me.* Maggie, laughing then. Maggie liked to be scared . . .

"He's not going to tell me he's too busy to come to see me," Ellen said.

"He might. So be prepared. I know he was friendly at John's funeral. It was plain he was glad to talk to you. But that was a special situation. Things are back to normal now. And you remember the way he used to be. Not exactly social. And maybe he hasn't changed that much. Besides, it could be painful for him. If you keep talking about Maggie. That was a bad time in his life, mom. He might not want to remember."

"Of course, it's painful. But how can that matter?"

"Because it's pain and it hurts. That's how it can matter. And nobody likes it, wants it, goes in search of it." Liz was about to add, *At least sane people don't,* but she stopped herself in time. Even so, the unspoken words hung in the air.

Ellen seemed to ignore the words. "He loved Maggie," she said softly.

Liz remembered how Maggie had laughed over that love, eyes alight, cheeks dimpling. *He'd do anything for me, Liz. Oh, it's fun, you wouldn't know, to tease him on, and see it happen, and feel him poking up at me, as if I'm a magnet and he can't help himself . . .*

Liz spoke tonelessly. "Yes. I guess he did love her. But that was a long time ago."

"Time doesn't matter," Ellen said. "He's never married."

"He's only twenty-nine. And sometimes men don't marry until later. You know that. You're just trying to convince yourself . . ."

"Maggie's twenty-seven. Just right. The two of them together . . ."

"Mom! Please stop it!" Softly, within her mind, Liz spoke to herself. *Run. Get out of here. Let her rave if she has to. Just don't listen.* But where was she to run to, Liz asked herself, arguing the soft voice into silence. And how could she leave her mother alone?

"Of course he never married," Ellen said thoughtfully. "Because of Maggie. How could he? Remembering her."

"Naturally he remembers her, but that doesn't mean . . ."

"So you see?"

"How could he have forgotten her?" Liz asked tartly. "After what happened."

Ellen turned the wheelchair and slowly rolled herself away. She didn't want to hear any more. She had learned to protect herself against Liz's disbelief.

It was the only way Ellen could go on. Otherwise life would be too painful to bear. Day after day, empty. Night after night, and fearful dreams. Liz had a closed mind, a closed heart. She didn't understand. She didn't want to understand. . . .

Maggie was there, lingering in the shadows. Waiting. Maggie had never really gone away altogether. She was waiting to come back.

And now that Claude was here, Ellen was convinced that Maggie would soon show herself. Claude's love and her mother's love would draw her from the dark into the light.

Ellen knew that she had been weak, faithless, over the years. She would talk to Maggie days and nights, believing, hoping and then, feeling Liz's disapproval, she would stop, hide belief, bury hope. She would pretend that she had forgotten. But no more. Never again. Now Claude was back it would be different. He would understand her and believe in her. He would give her

113

his young man's strength. And so together they would make Maggie hear.

The big front room had once been her husband Morgan's den, and that was where he had worked over his briefs long after Ellen had gone to bed. Gone to bed to lie alone and dream of love. . . .

She wheeled herself so that she could look out of the window. She didn't realize that Liz had followed her until she heard Liz asking, "Do you want to watch television?"

Ellen shook her head.

"Want a book?"

"No, thanks." Ellen smiled faintly. "Don't worry, Liz. I'm all right."

"Call me if you want something."

"I will."

"The bell's right there."

Ellen smiled again. "I know, Liz. I know. I'm just fine." She watched Liz walk to the door, hesitate, then disappear into the hallway. Step firm. Shoulders straight. Chestnut head high. A good girl. A loving daughter. It was hard for her, and she did the best she could. But there was so much she didn't know.

Ellen leaned back, looked out of the window. It framed a view of the front gardens and the driveway. The lawns were overgrown and weed filled. The once shapely bushes had swelled to grotesque outlines.

As she watched, the present faded. . . . She saw herself walking slowly along the path through carefully tended grounds. Her dress was pink, full at the skirt, and short enough to reveal the long slender legs beneath. She was breathless, hurrying. But suddenly she stopped. Maggie was there. Smiling. She moved in quick dancing steps, her arms outflung to

114

embrace the world eagerly. Her red miniskirt came to mid-thigh. Her white blouse was tight enough over her uptilted breasts to show the peak of her nipples beneath it. Morgan had always protested. But Maggie had only laughed and gone her own way. Maggie at seventeen, sweet, laughing Maggie, whose whole life was before her on that August day.

Ellen watched her disappear into the house, then went on, walking quickly between the tall iron gates. Outside, her step slowed. She knew there wasn't much time, but uneasiness burdened her. A tone in Dane's quiet words. An edge of excite-ment that troubled her. She went slowly through the sunny August morning until, at the place where the road ended in a bank of shining trees, she saw the familiar car. Then she forced herself to hurry again. Dane was waiting for her.

Dane was waiting. She put her uneasiness aside and hurried to him. That was the beginning. Or the end. The end she refused to believe in.

He leaned forward, welcoming her. His face, partly in sun, partly in shadow, was unaccountably sober. Sudden pulses of alarm tapped at her temples. If she was troubled before, she was frightened now. "What is it?" she asked breathlessly, whis-pering, although there was no one but him to hear her.

"We need to talk. Do you have time now?"

"Yes. I think so. Morgan's gone to the county seat this morning. He'll be there most of the day. Maggie's at home. And Liz went fishing early." Her small family, all accounted for, placed properly where each belonged. She was free.

Dane began to speak quickly, his voice gruff. "We can't go on like this."

Her alarm faced, and she sagged back. She was almost re-sentful that he'd frightened her for nothing. Without consciously thinking about it, she'd begun to imagine unfaceable possibilities. Morgan knew. Morgan had spoken to Dane.

She hadn't meant to fall in love with him. It had been sudden, unplanned. They'd known each other for years as good friends. Dane and Morgan played golf together; Dane came for dinner once a week. The three of them took occasional trips. She was a young forty-five. Gay. Just a little flirtatious. It amused her to have two men dancing attendance on her. She was pleased by the looks of envy her escorts evoked. Dane's gallantries made up for Morgan's preoccupations.

On one of the trips, when Morgan was sleeping late, as he preferred to do when on vacation, she had gone out, walking into the beach sunrise. Dane had caught up with her. He took her by the hand, saying, out of nowhere and out of nothing, it seemed, "Ellen, do you have any idea of what I feel for you? Do you realize how hard it is for me to hide it? I can't pretend any longer. I can't hold it in any more."

Suddenly she had felt the same. She'd never thought of it before. It had never crossed her mind. But in that instant she was transformed. She didn't know why. She didn't know how. It had simply happened. Perhaps because Morgan was an old fifty-seven. And Dane was a young fifty-two. And she was alive. So alive.

She had looked into his eyes and softly said his name. Just that. His name. Then his arms were around her, his lips touched hers. First gently. Finally with passion. Red morning sun bathed them as they sank to the sand together. They promised each other, later, that it would never happen again. They would go on as before. Friends. But the promises were broken within days, and they made no more vain vows.

For the past year they had met secretly. It was difficult in

116

Meadowville. But they managed. When they met in public it was the same as it had been before. They met in private as often as they safely could, for stolen moments, stolen caresses. Sometimes an hour by day. But more often in the night. Morgan was often away on the circuit. He slept soundly when he was at home. Once, slipping out, she had thought herself discovered. There had been a stir close by where she passed. Maggie? Liz? She had never been sure. It had troubled her that one of the girls might be creeping out at night. But she never dared inquire. She told herself it must have been her imagination.

It could have gone on that way. Ellen felt only slight guilt. She had been deprived for years of love. Now she had found it. She took nothing from Morgan, who didn't want her, when she gave to Dane, who did.

But Dane needed more than a surreptitious love affair. He needed a wife again. Since he had lost Clara he'd had no one. Now he had Ellen. He demanded all of her. All her love, all her time, all her attentions. But how could she be what he needed? There was Maggie and Liz and Morgan. They were there, and wanted her, too.

Yet Dane was insistent. "We have to do something, Ellen. You can divorce Morgan. The girls are nearly grown. They can manage. My John's a man. Claude is too. Or should be, even if he isn't. They'd be all right, if you divorced and we married."

It frightened her. She'd known he was thinking it, but to hear him say it aloud . . . divorce. And all Meadowville would know. She was a Paige. He was a Vickery. They stood for something in the town. They *were* the town.

"Ellen, will you?"

She was too frightened even to think. The words came out,

unplanned. "No, Dane. No, no. I couldn't. You know I couldn't. And neither could you."

"Suppose we went away . . ." His voice was very soft, tender. "The two of us . . . South America, for instance. New lives together . . ."

"And how are we to go away?" She'd held him tightly. "How could we? Let's be happy with what we have, Dane."

It was an argument they'd had many times before. It always ended in lovemaking.

Now, as she sat beside him in the car, he didn't reach for her, but continued to speak. "We can't go on like this. I'm tired of it. And so are you. We don't have to live this way. Not any more. I've taken care of the future for us. I've finally *made* the future for us, Ellen."

Her Dane. Virile. Driving. How she wanted him then. She moved closer, whispered, "Dane. Not now. Not again. We've spoken of it so often. And it's no use."

"We can leave. Go to South America. In Brazil we'll never see anybody from here. We can build new lives among strangers. Together."

"Dane!"

"Ellen, listen to me. We have the money. We can pack this afternoon. We can be in St. Louis in a few hours, and on a plane. In no time we'd leave the past behind us for good."

"What are you talking about?" she had cried. "What do you mean? Fly away. Leave. Disappear into a strange world forever." She was frightened. It was one thing to talk of it, dream of it, plan it, wish for it, always regretting that it couldn't be. It was something else when the dreaming became reality. All she knew was Meadowville. Dead Man's Bluff. St. Louis. All she knew was her children. Morgan. Her friends.

And Dane. Dane, her lover. But if they went away together, left everything else behind, then what would she have?

"I have the money. I told you," Dane had said. "It took me a few months. But I've been working at it. Ever since I realized you and I love each other." A grim smile touched his lips. "Being president of the bank helped of course."

"What did you do?" she asked breathlessly.

"You needn't know the details."

She sat silent, shivering in the autumn heat. It seemed as if an abyss yawned before her. A fearful future in a faraway land. No familiar landmarks to guide her. No one but Dane to love her. "Just go?" she said at last, wonderingly. "Leave and never see the girls again? Never see Morgan?"

"For me. With me."

"And the same for you," she went on. "You'd be giving up everything."

"For you. I want to, Ellen."

She didn't know how to answer him.

But he knew even before she finally found the words. He saw it in her face, in her denying eyes. He could feel her sliding away from him even though she didn't move.

"No?" he asked. "After all we've said? Just no?"

"I couldn't. We couldn't."

"But it's done," he'd said softly.

"Done? What do you mean it's done?"

"I told you. I have the money. In cash."

She was still close to him, their bodies touching at shoulder and hip and thigh. Close as they always sat, when they were alone. But she felt as if a wall had grown up between them. The warm summer sun had a sudden edge of chill, and the sun-speckled shadows had all at once become ominous. "Dane, we

119

can't do it. You must return the money to the bank at once."

"I couldn't. Not without telling them what I've done. Telling the board. And Morgan."

"But there's no other way. I couldn't let you become a criminal for me. A hunted man. And the butt of Meadowville's malice. No, no. I couldn't."

"I'm already a criminal," he said softly. "And I'll soon bear the malice."

"Not if you give the money back."

"You won't come with me?"

"I can't."

"Then you and I . . . we were never really anything to each other?"

"We were. We are. I'll always love you," she said. But it was only words. Meaningless reassurance. She knew it, and so did he.

"You won't change your mind, Ellen?"

"How can I?" she asked despairingly. "You ask me to turn my back on my life, Dane."

"Yes," he agreed. "It's a lot, isn't it?" He kissed her lightly. "All right then. I'll do as you say."

"And we go on as before." But she didn't think they would. It wouldn't be possible. She would never feel the same about him. It was too big a risk. He would ask too much, demand too much. Whatever she had once felt for him was gone now. It hadn't been love. She finally understood that. It had been something else. She didn't want to give a name to it. She repeated, "Yes, we'll go on as before."

But the next evening the phone rang and, unsuspecting, she answered it. Morgan was calling. He sounded unlike himself, strange, asking how she was, if she were alone. When she said she was fine and that the girls were somewhere around the house, he went on. "Ellen, something terrible has happened to Dane. He's dead."

For the next two days she walked as if in a dream. The tears she spilled were taken to be the tears shed for a friend. When she trembled at Dane's graveside, Morgan supported her, himself red eyed and shaking.

The whole town, all the mourners at the cemetery, knew what Dane had done. That he'd embezzled from the bank, had had a change of heart and returned the money, and had committed suicide because he couldn't face his shame. The whole town knew his guilt, but not hers.

That night, late, the doorbell rang. The police were there with the news that Maggie was dead. Maggie, who should have been asleep in her room upstairs. Maggie, the beautiful, the well loved. Maggie.

Ellen had collapsed, screaming. Her auburn hair turned white within weeks. Her face quickly wrinkled with the loss of flesh, her round cheeks fell in, the bright smile dimmed.

Morgan became nothing beyond a pale wraith to her, shouldering the burden of her collapse and the loss of Maggie. He lasted three years, then died on the bench while hearing the case of a drunken driver charged with involuntary homicide. Liz became Ellen's mainstay. Liz, and the slowly evolving belief that Maggie would return.

She couldn't be dead and gone forever. Her mother's love could rescue her from the limbo in which she wandered.

When Ellen learned that Claude was returning to town, she took it to be the sign she had been waiting for, working toward. Now that Claude was there, Maggie would soon be, too . . . .

Outside there was a sound. A car rolled up the driveway and stopped. A tall, hunched figure stepped out and stood looking up at the house.

Ellen raised her head and smiled. It was Claude Vickery. She had willed him here. She had willed him to come to her. And he had come.

He took off his glasses, shoved them into his jacket and came slowly toward the verandah. The sun, shining behind him, formed a nimbus around his body. And walking next to him, dancing along in a miniskirt, Ellen could almost see Maggie. Almost . . .

He was suddenly standing in the doorway. Ellen hadn't heard the doorbell ring. She hadn't heard Liz greet him. But it didn't matter.

She sat up. "Claude, welcome. Come in."

"I hope I'm not disturbing you. Maybe I ought to have called first. But I was just passing by, and I thought, maybe, for just a minute . . ."

It wasn't true. He hadn't just been passing by. He'd been thinking of coming here ever since he'd suddenly found himself in front of the house. And before that, he'd been thinking about it, though he wasn't really aware of it. Today, he made the decision. He wouldn't call and ask for permission. Suppose he was told that he oughtn't to come? He would just appear. The worst that could happen would be that the door was closed in his face. And the door hadn't been closed against him. Liz had looked him up and down, her hot blue eyes expressionless. She'd waved him in, not speaking.

But now she said, "Your timing is good, Claude. My mother was talking about giving you a call just a little while ago."

"Yes," Ellen agreed. "I was going to ask you to dinner. Perhaps you knew?"

He gave her a confused look. "Knew? As I said, I was just passing by . . ."

Ellen waved his words away. She suggested to Liz that he might want tea, asked if there were cookies. She told Claude to come and sit close beside her.

He did as told, lurching in his awkward walk to a chair. Then, looking at Liz, he said, "Nothing for me, thank you. Nothing. I don't want to be any trouble." He just managed to get the words out. The stammer was on him again. He took a deep breath and looked at the green love seat. He remembered it from long before. He and Maggie used to sit there together while Judge Paige talked about the antiwar demonstrations on the college campuses, and asked Claude if he was involved in them. And Maggie had laughed, *Oh, papa, don't be silly. Why would Claude . . .*

Liz, murmuring something, went out and left him alone with Ellen Paige.

Her eyes were very bright and there was a touch of color in both cheeks. "Oh, it's good to see you here, Claude."

He gave her a look of relief, thinking of Liz's coldness. In the hall, as she was bringing him to the front room, he'd said quickly, "Liz, I know you told me not to come. But I *had* to. To talk to your mother. Just for a little while. But you'd better tell me the truth. Is it okay? For her? If she'd rather not see me . . ."

Liz had been cool but honest. "She wants you, Claude. So I guess it'll have to be okay."

But now, standing in the kitchen where she had gone to

escape, Liz thought that it wasn't okay. No, it could never be okay. Claude's arrival could do nothing but reawaken Ellen's memories. Memories best left dormant, if not altogether buried. Not just Ellen's memories either. But Liz's own.

She put water on to boil, then sat at the table to make up a shopping list. But soon her pencil no longer moved across the paper. For years she hadn't allowed herself to remember. What good would it have done? But now she was forced to it. It was as if Maggie had come back to take stage center again. It was the worst thing that could happen to Ellen. Anything that made her concentrate even more on Maggie could only harm her. She was already so frail from having given away ten years of her life to grief. And ten years of Liz's life as well . . .

For an instant Liz faced her own bitterness. What Maggie's death had done to her. And all because of Claude. Why had Maggie gone with him that night? She'd said she was tired of him. She'd said he was too intense. She'd said it didn't really matter because there was always Red. But she'd gone.

She hadn't come back alive.

It seemed to Liz that her own life had ended that night too. And all because of Claude.

Because of Claude. If only Richard hadn't tried to locate him. If only Richard had understood what it might mean for her mother, for Liz herself.

Meanwhile, in the front room Ellen leaned back in her chair. "Let me have a good look at you, Claude."

He smiled tentatively. "I don't think there's much to look at. I'm still pretty much the same, I guess."

"Ah, no. You've changed. You're all grown up."

"Maybe. But I wasn't really a child when . . . when . . . it happened."

124

"Not a child," she agreed. "But ten years is a long time. You're a man now."

He said nothing. He wondered if her grief over Maggie's death had whitened her hair, put those deep lines in her face. He wondered when she had lost the use of her legs, and why. But he was careful not to ask. He supposed he'd soon find out. Someone else would tell him. There was a lot of catching up to do, but there was time for it. He was already beginning to think that the two years ahead stretched out into forever. When he first decided to come back he'd had the half-formed idea that he'd leave as soon as the time was up. He would get through it, and be done. Now he'd forgotten that.

"Do you think of her often?" Ellen asked.

Her. Maggie. Did he? Always. Always. There was no moment when she wasn't in his mind. It was why he'd come back to Meadowville. So he could be closer to her. He tried to speak, and choked. It took a long, slow moment before he could manage to conquer the stammer. At last he said, "Yes, Mrs. Paige. I do."

"So do I," she answered. "Always." After a little while, she asked, "And is it because of her that you never married?"

He wanted to change the subject. It couldn't be good for Mrs. Paige to sit and talk of Maggie. To look at him, to think of her lost daughter. But he had to answer the question. "I think so. Probably," he said, and saw that it was true. Before he hadn't been certain. There had been girls. He'd been serious about two of them. Neither had worked out. He supposed he hadn't allowed them to work out.

"Ah, yes," Ellen sighed. "I can understand. A first love. So strong. So real." She looked directly at him. "I hope you haven't given up hope. You mustn't, you know."

He didn't know what to say. He took out his glasses and stuck them on his nose. The lenses were smudged. Her face seemed blurred, the room suddenly cloudy. He wiped sweat from his brow.

She went on. "Maggie's very close now. I nearly saw her walking beside you on the path."

Ellen didn't notice that he jumped a little, didn't see that first he jumped as if struck, and then froze.

He tried to answer her, to say, *What? What do you mean?* but couldn't utter the words, although he heard them in his head.

"It won't be long," she said, "if you want to help me, Claude."

After too long a pause he answered. "Help you, Mrs. Paige?"

"Help me call Maggie. You see, I'm sure she hears me. I'm sure she's out there, waiting. Perhaps it's been you that she's been waiting for."

He didn't answer. Fear had him by the throat. A chill wind blew inside his head. He blinked, swallowed, struggled for breath. He'd thought when he heard her speak of Maggie as close by she'd only meant that it was a feeling, a memory. But now she'd said she could almost see her. *See* her?

"You think I'm crazy, don't you," Ellen asked. There was a smile on her face. She didn't look upset. "It's all right. I understand. I guess you've heard about it. At least from Liz. Maybe even from Richard. All of them. They talk, of course. They'll tell you that I mumble to myself and think I'm talking to spirits from the other side. They'll tell you I see things. Apparitions. But it's only because they can't help themselves. They don't want to believe. They're scared to believe." She took a quick, panting breath. "But there's nothing to fear.

Maggie loved us. And we loved her. She'll come back to us soon. I'll see Maggie again. I'll hear her voice. I know that. I know it, Claude. And so will you." Ellen smiled. "That is, if you loved her, love her still, then so will you."

He was speechless, shivering. He seemed to be sinking in her words, drowning in them. He felt as if a will stronger than his own had seized him, held him. After a long time, he spoke, his voice thin as a whisper. "I never stopped loving Maggie. I guess I've never really believed she was dead."

He left before Liz brought in the tea. He forgot that he had driven over, and when he was outside the house, he broke into a run. He didn't stop until he got home.

Red Stanton and his crew were working.

Claude raced upstairs. He had to be alone. He had to think, to sort it out. He had to get hold of himself.

But Red's voice was pounding in his ears. "What's the matter with him?"

There would be more. More, and Claude couldn't stand it. He flung himself down on the bed and pulled a pillow over his head.

Chapter 10

That night Richard and Liz were in the Hilton Hide-away. They sat close together on a blue velveteen banquette, but took no comfort in the contact.

Richard's face had its stubborn look—his jaw squared, his mouth firm. There was a flush on Liz's cheeks, and her blue eyes shone hot under her dark brows.

"If you could have seen him . . . the expression on his face when he passed me, not even knowing I was there. And he left his car. Just started out running, as if he had a dozen ghosts at his heels. I went in and asked mom. Expecting she'd be upset too. But no, and that's funny, I think, she said she was fine. She said they'd been talking. And he suddenly got up and told her he had to go. But he'd come back."

"Maybe he didn't feel well."

"Richard! Really, sometimes I wonder what's wrong with you."

"Probably plenty." He forced a grin. "But I think you're building it up out of proportion. Claude came for a visit. He

128

and your mother had a chat. He went home. That's how I see it." He went on quickly as Liz started to speak. "I realize he can be pretty gauche some times. But so what? Nobody's perfect."

She shook her head. Without moving, she seemed to have separated herself from Richard. He didn't like the feeling he had. He was alone, adrift. He took her hand. As he saw it, the trouble was that she just didn't want Claude Vickery around.

Liz put the thought into words. "I don't want him here, Richard. I don't want him anywhere around my mother, or around me."

Richard uneasily considered her words. What was there to do? Talk to Claude about it? Say frankly what Liz was telling him?

"And the things I find myself thinking," she burst out. "Honestly, Richard. I don't know where they come from. But they actually scare me!"

"Scare you? Aren't you overdoing it just a little?" he asked gently.

"Maybe I am. I don't know any more." Her hot eyes met his. "But sometimes I find myself wishing the Vickery house would burn down." A small shiver moved her shoulders. "So Claude would have to go away."

"Liz, come on."

She whispered, "And I think of silly, crazy, childish tricks. Oh, God, I don't know what's happening to me."

He took both her hands into his. "Nothing is happening to you. You're concerned about your mother. You're building up Claude's importance, and looking for trouble that isn't there."

"He's trouble. And he's here," she said. But she didn't tell Richard any more . . . How, for instance, she had wondered through half the day what would happen if she did a tape of her mother's voice, whispering to Maggie, and then stuck it somehow into Claude's stereo. She didn't mention how she'd found herself suddenly thinking about sending Claude an anonymous note. A warning of danger. A threat. Before she'd stopped herself, she had almost planned the wording, the means to do it, too. She'd been disgusted. Upset. The ugliness of the fantasies bothered her. She'd tried to work it off by raking leaves. Then she'd called Mrs. Baldwin, and made arrangements to spend the evening with Richard . . .

But now she wished that she hadn't. She had only the one thing on her mind, and Richard didn't understand. Nor did he even seem to want to.

She finished her drink. "I want to go home."

He didn't argue. He paid the bill, got up with her. But he wasn't planning to take her home. They'd stop first at his house. They'd have another drink. He wanted to hold her in his arms until she relaxed, until she was herself again. He wanted to make love to her. Maybe, by then, she'd want it, too.

But when he suggested it, she said, "No. Not tonight."

"Why not tonight? We don't have all that many chances."

"It's how I feel, Richard."

He jerked the car to a stop, turned to her. "Listen, are you punishing me? Is that it?"

It was direct, the way he wanted it to be. Get it out into the open. Make her say it.

But she playacted instead. "Punishing you? What for? No. It's just the mood I'm in."

"You're ducking," Richard said. "You're mad at me for getting Claude back. You're blaming me."

"No." But there was little conviction in her voice. "I realize

130

it wasn't your fault. Not really. It was John." The words resounded with open doubt.

"I did what I had to do," he said. "And I'm not sorry."

When she didn't answer, he drove on. He let the silence go on until he pulled up before his house. "Want to have a drink with me?" he asked, as if she hadn't refused before.

"All right," she said. "Just one."

After they'd had several drinks, she suddenly put her glass aside, and went to him. She burrowed her head into his shoulder and whispered, "Richard, I'm sorry. I didn't mean it."

He knew she had meant it, but he didn't say so. He held her tightly until she wriggled away, laughing, to race him into the bedroom.

Later, when they were dressing, he thought of saying, *Let's not waste any more time, Liz. Let's get married and see how it goes.* But knowing what she would say, he held the words back.

Red Stanton arrived at the Hilton Hide-away a few minutes after Richard and Liz had gone.

He settled at the bar, sourly dismissing his surroundings. The Hide-away wasn't his usual drinking place. Mostly he went to the Glass Slipper. But he hadn't felt like going there that night. He'd wanted to sit by himself, to think and not be distracted by having his war buddies' jokes banging away in the background.

He and June had had another argument. He'd stamped out, glad of the excuse even though he never needed one. He couldn't remember what started it. Maybe nothing had. Sometimes he just looked at June and felt his temper coming up. Tonight he was knotty, on edge. Something had to give, though he didn't know what. It was working at Claude's, he guessed. He kept thinking of Maggie. And how she had died. And how Claude was pretending, now that he was back, that nothing had happened. But Claude was cracked. There was no doubt about that. If he wasn't, he'd never have returned to Meadowville. No matter what.

Red leaned both elbows on the counter and ordered another beer. When the bartender, Pete Burger, brought it, saying something about the weather, Red ignored the pleasantry. The seed which Vernon Meese had planted had taken root; Red didn't even remember where he had gotten the idea, but he sat there, thinking again, about how he could fix up the Vickery house so it could be a recreation center for the kids, and about the best way to hit the Council of Aldermen for enough money to get it furnished right.

Meanwhile, Pete Burger, seeing that Red wasn't going to talk, drifted to the other end of the bar. "Want anything else?" he asked of the small blond girl who sat there by herself."

"Not yet, but thanks," she answered, smiling.

"Just whistle when you do." He liked her. He liked the way her long blond hair flowed down her back. He liked the way she was quiet, and kept to herself, and never looked at the guys. She let them know she wasn't available so there were no mistakes for him to untangle. And he liked her smile. It was friendly, just a little bit timid. He wasn't sure how long she'd been around, or what she was doing in Meadowville. He hoped she was planning to stay on. Not that it would mean anything to him. He was sixty-three, and had five kids, and a wife that kept him happy at home. It was just that he liked the looks of the small blond girl.

But the girl whose name was Dina Forrest was thinking

about leaving. She'd had a good rest in Meadowville, had stretched her legs and gotten the travel dust out of her lungs, exploring the quiet streets until she'd begun to feel almost at home. And she liked the town. It seemed pleasant to her, almost familiar. But there was nothing to stay for. And San Francisco still beckoned. As she sat at the bar she decided to call the bus depot and find out the schedule. She'd check out first thing in the morning.

When she paid Pete she told him that she was leaving, and was surprised at his look of disappointment. On the way back to her room she changed her mind, and decided to take one last walk.

Even though it was cool, the outside air felt good on her face. She huddled inside her suit jacket as she cut through the parking lot to the street.

It was ten o'clock and very quiet. There was no one about and nothing moving. Yet neither the silence nor the emptiness bothered her. Dina had already sized up Meadowville as a town where nothing much happened.

But suddenly, inexplicably, she felt as if she were being watched. She could sense eyes on her. Her flesh began to crawl, as if strange fingertips were stroking it.

The alarm flooded through her in a quick hot wave. She cast quick glances behind her, then ahead. No. There was still nothing, no one. But without knowing why, without even thinking about it, she turned back.

She hurried around a pickup truck, looking ahead to the lights of the Hilton side entrance which, as she looked at them, disappeared. She saw nothing before her. No lights. No building. She heard no sound.

But she felt a wrenching. A jostling. She stopped. Yet even then she felt as if she were being pulled one way, shoved another.

Her body seemed to be caving in and exploding outward at the same time. She gasped without air, struggled without strength.

In instants it was over. She dropped to the ground, her purse beneath her prone body, and was still.

Half an hour later Red Stanton found her.

Earlier that same night Ellen Paige sighed in her sleep and turned and sighed again. She lay high on two pillows, a blue blanket drawn up around her shoulders, the small silver bell just beyond her outflung hand. The drapes were drawn, but a single ray of moonlight filtered through a crack. In the outside stillness, a pair of blue jays suddenly began to complain. They were easily heard in the hush of the shadow-filled room. Ellen breathed deeply, turned once more. After a moment, she awakened.

She lay quietly, listening. Someone had called to her, she thought. Called, *Mother, mother.* There was nothing now but faint echoes of it. *Mother, mother.* But she had heard it. She was sure. And it had to be Maggie. It could only be Maggie. Liz always called her mom. And Liz wouldn't awaken her from a sound sleep. No. It was Maggie.

Slowly, almost afraid to, Ellen opened her eyes and raised her head. "Maggie, is that you?"

The answer came, words and a sweet, soft laugh. "Yes, mother. I'm here."

The small girl with flaming hair sat on the nearby love seat, slender legs crossed, one foot gently swinging. A thin shaft of light fell on her face. Her heavy-lidded eyes sparkled like gems. Her teeth flashed.

"Is it true?" Ellen asked wonderingly. "Is this happening? Are you real? Or am I dreaming? Have I gone mad, as they say I am."

"I'm here," Maggie said. "How come you're acting so surprised?"

"No." Ellen was breathless. "No, I'm not surprised." She held out her arms. "I always knew you'd come back. I've waited so long, prayed so long."

Maggie sat still, ignoring her mother's reaching arms. "I know. You'd be astonished at what I know. What I've always known." Behind her words were myriad layers of meaning.

Ellen didn't notice. She flicked tears from her eyes. "Dear God, I can't believe it has really happened. I always knew it would, but I still can't believe it."

Maggie laughed again.

"Was it Claude that brought you?" Ellen asked. "Was it Claude after all?" Plainly she was hoping to have another answer. Her face begged for it.

But Maggie shrugged. "Oh, Claude, yes. And you too." The laughter was gone. The sweetness of the smile faded. Maggie leaned forward. "Did you really think that no one knew?" she asked softly. "Did you honestly believe that you had gotten away with it for good?"

"Knew?" Ellen asked. "Knew what?"

"About you and Dane Vickery."

Ellen gasped, couldn't speak. Once when she had slipped out to meet Dane she'd thought she felt someone watching, listening. Someone who had also slipped out. Liz. Maggie. Ellen had never tried to find out, had been afraid to. Now it no longer mattered . . .

"It's time to pay, mother," Maggie said. "Nothing comes for free."

Ellen stared, her breath rasping in her throat.

"For you. But, of course, for Claude too."

"He loves you. He always loved you," Ellen choked out.

"Oh, did he?"

"And I loved you."

"But you loved yourself much more."

"No, no, Maggie. You don't understand."

"I do."

"Maggie . . ."

"How touchingly you say my name," Maggie jeered. "It must have been a comfort to you all these years to hear your voice."

"Maggie . . ."

The girl got up. She moved slowly, as if she were dancing a pavane to silent music. In long langorous steps she came to stand at her mother's bedside. "Why don't you take your silver bell and ring for Liz?"

Ellen didn't answer. But she couldn't have called for Liz. She had no strength. No breath.

"Is it because Liz can't help you now?" The jeer was back in Maggie's voice. "For all she's done for you, playing good daughter, she can't do anything any more."

Ellen gathered herself, made words, whispered them. "You sound so strange. Claude loved you. We all did. Everybody in town. It was terrible when you died."

"It was terrible for me."

136

"Yes. How well I knew that. How often I imagined it. We all suffered with you. And poor Claude, his mind broke under the strain. He couldn't . . ."

"But he lived," Maggie cut in. "You all lived and survived, even with your pain. I was the only one who died." She laughed softly. "At least it seemed that way to me. I was the only one. But of course Dane Vickery died, too."

"And the day he was buried, you and Claude . . ."

"That's right, mother. It was really your fault. All of it. Right from the beginning. You always were a silly, vain woman. You and your pretty dresses, and narrow waist, and painted finger-nails. You always the belle of the ball. If you hadn't flirted with Dane, and led him on, and turned his head, and twisted his heart around and then dropped him when he stole for you . . . if you hadn't killed Dane Vickery as surely as if you'd pulled the gun's trigger yourself, then I'd never have been in that car with Claude. We'd never have been driving on Dead Man's Bluff."

"Maggie . . . Maggie . . . my love . . ."

"You shouldn't have brought me back if you didn't want the truth, mother. After all, I can't lie now. And why would I want to."

"I want the truth. But I can't bear . . . I can't bear . . ." Breath burned like acid in Ellen's throat. Weight throbbed and pounded in her chest. "I can't bear . . ."

"The word you won't say is guilt. And you have to bear what's yours to bear. Whatever happens. Just as I did."

"Forgive," Ellen whispered breathlessly. "Forgive me, Maggie."

"Why should I? You're alive, aren't you? And Claude is too."

"You say that as if you wished . . . wished for the both of us to have died. Don't you realize how he's suffered? What it has meant to him . . . the loss of you?"

"Not enough, mother. Not yet. But he will." Maggie laughed softly. "I'll see to that."

"Then what have I done? I loved you back and brought you back because I couldn't bear to be without you. And now I hear hate in your voice, and see it in your eyes."

"You can't change what's there, mother. You never knew me, you only thought you did."

"Knew you? What a strange thing to say. Of course I knew you. You were my own little girl."

Maggie laughed shrilly. "Oh, boy. What an act. Even now you're playacting. You saw what you wanted to see. You, the others too. You wanted a sweet, laughing and happy Maggie. So that's what you thought I was. But there was something more to me, mother. Fire. Ice. A little hell raging inside."

"Yes," Ellen whispered. "I think I guessed at that."

"And wouldn't risk facing it. Because you were afraid."

"Because I loved you, wanted to protect you."

"That won't save you." The girl bent over Ellen. "Nothing can save you from what you've done."

"Maggie," Ellen cried breathlessly, "Oh, my Maggie . . ."

Liz found her early in the morning. She lay high on the pillows, clasping the silver bell in her cold hands. Her eyes were wide, her blue lips drawn back in a grimace of anguish.

Weeping, Liz ran for the phone.

Chapter 11

Four days later Claude stood at the fringes of the crowd, watching as Ellen Paige was laid to rest in the site reserved for her between her husband Morgan and her older daughter Maggie.

His head bowed, he remembered his last visit with her and how she had spoken of Maggie, and Maggie's returning and how, at the last, he had fled from her certainty in mixed terror and hope.

Both the terror he hadn't understood and the hope he had cherished were gone now. They had died in him when he learned that Ellen Paige was dead.

He ignored the others at the graveside. Vernon Meese and his wife. Willie Harker. Red Stanton with June. After a single quick glance at Liz, standing rigidly next to Richard, Claude kept his eyes fixed on the leaf-strewn ground at his feet.

When the services were over, and the others left, he hung back until he was alone. Long after the hum of the cars had faded away into the afternoon stillness he stood there, unmoving, his eyes fixed on the ground. Finally he went down to his knees on the raw uncovered earth that was Ellen's grave, the moist loamy soil so soft that it packed under his weight and he seemed almost to sink into it. His gaze settled on the white monument that marked Maggie's place, and he spoke.

"I'm sorry for everything, Maggie. I wish it could have been different."

From far away a robin called. A sudden wind stirred the limbs of the leafless trees.

"God, how I miss you." He buried his face in his hands.

Willie Harker, watching the scene, backed quietly away from the yews that had sheltered him and trotted to his car.

Later that afternoon, just four days after she had fallen in the shadows of the Hilton parking lot, the girl named Dina Forrest stirred and opened her eyes. She stared blankly at the pale yellow walls. He body was sore. Her mind was empty.

A smiling face suddenly hovered over her, and she looked blankly into it. Who was this? What was that thing on her head?

The nurse was young, pretty and plainly very pleased. She had a clean bright smile and dimples. Her white, starched ruffle stood up on her black curls. She said, "Ms. Forrest. Dina, if you don't mind. Hello, and welcome back."

Dina asked thickly, "What happened?"

"The truth is, you were beginning to worry us. It took so long. But here you are again. Don't worry. You're okay. Everything's all right."

"But where am I?" Dina asked. "I don't understand. Something's awfully wrong." And in a frightened rush, "Who is Ms. Forrest? Or Dina? Or whatever it was you called me?"

140

The nurse's smile faded. A small frown grew between her brows. But she said reassuringly, "Now don't worry. It's all right. You've had a blow to the head. That's why your memory's playing tricks on you. It happens that way sometimes. But it'll pass in a little while. Suppose you just close your eyes and rest, and I'll ring for the doctor."

"Wait, wait. Don't go away. Just tell me. Who is this Forrest person. And where am I? And what's going on?"

"Rest," the nurse answered. Before Dina could protest further or ask more questions, the nurse swept out of the room.

Rest. What a strange thing to say under the circumstances. The nurse looked to her as if she might have been intelligent, but she certainly didn't talk as if she were. How could Dina rest? As she raised her head from the pillow, the room suddenly seemed to spin around. The pale walls began to darken. No good. Dina lay back again. The pounding was terrible. The questions were terrible, too. Where was she? What had happened? And damn it—Oh, damn it all to hell, why had that nurse called her Dina Forrest? The name meant nothing to her. Nothing. *Nothing.*

In that instant Dina realized, for the first time, that the nurse called her that thinking she was someone named Dina Forrest. Of course. Why hadn't she realized this before? But that was impossible. There was some silly mistake. Dina Forrest wasn't her name. How could it be? It meant absolutely nothing to her. But then . . . then what *was* her name? Who was she? And what was she doing in a hospital with a nurse bending over her? Come to that, *where* was she?

Frightened and bewildered, she tried to turn her head. Her neck felt full of rocks. The pounding in her head worsened, and everything ached. Her ribs. Shoulders. The bones in her hands.

Her knees. Her ankles. She felt bruised all over. She lay still, her eyes closed, and tried to imagine what she looked like. Everybody in the world had some idea of how they must look. But she didn't. Not the faintest glimmer came to her. God. God. Hot tears burned her eyes, crept from beneath the closed lids to slide down her pale cheeks. It was impossible. It was the most terrible feeling. She couldn't imagine her own face. She didn't know her own name. With that came a recognition that frightened her even more. She didn't have even the faintest recollection of anything. No name. No past. And she didn't have any idea of where she was. She was in a pale yellow limbo. That was all. Something had happened to put her in a hospital. What that something was, she didn't know. She just didn't know . . .

"Ms. Forrest." The voice was deep, male.

Her eyes snapped open. "I was sleeping," she said irritably. "What's the idea?"

The doctor looked taken aback by her words.

But Dina looked even more so. "Oh, I'm sorry," she blurted. "I do need to talk to you. I don't know what's happening to me. You say my name is Dina Forrest. I don't recognize it. I'm obviously in a hospital. I can tell that. But how did I get here. And where is it? And what happened to me?"

"Let's take it slow and easy, shall we?"

"But I have to know." She heard the frantic note, and made herself stop or she knew she would start screaming. Something was wrong. She was scared. It kept getting worse. "Can't you tell me what happened?" she asked finally.

"Yes," he said, his voice soothing. "Of course. But first things first." He shushed her when she tried to speak. His examination was quick. He took her blood pressure, listened to her heart. Checked the pulses in her temples, the sides of her throat. With small metal hammers he tapped her shins, ankles, the bottoms of her feet. When he was finished, he said, "All right. Now we know a little more about where we stand. Heart's good. Blood pressure's a little high. But it would be. Reflexes are fine."

"And I have a terrible headache," she said.

"You ought to." He pulled out a chair, sat down. For a few moments he simply looked at her. Then he said, "You know, you're a pretty lucky girl."

"Lucky! What're you talking about?"

"You took a terrible blow to the head. At least that's what it seems like. But there's no fracture. No skin damaged. A bad concussion seems to be all you ended up with."

"And every bone in my body hurts."

"From the fall, I suppose. A bad blow; a bad fall. But you'll be all right."

"But what happened?"

His eyes fixed on hers. "That's what I was going to ask you. It's what the police will ask you as soon as I say they can see you."

In a hoarse whisper, she said, "I don't remember anything, doctor. Not even my own name."

"I see. That's what the nurse thought you said. Have you thought about it a little more? Maybe now . . ."

"There's nothing. My head's empty."

"Don't worry about it then. We've seen it before. It often follows after a knock on the head. Your memory will come back. It's only a matter of time."

He sounded so sure of himself that she sank back in relief. It was only later that she began to wonder how the nurse, the

143

doctor, had known what name to call her. . . .

A day passed, then another. Nothing happened. The name Dina Forrest never meant more to her than the first time she had heard it. Her mind remained empty. She had no past. She remembered nothing. She was like a baby newly born into a strange world. Gradually she learned what had happened. The police told her some of it, the doctor the rest.

She had been in a town called Meadowville for about five days, registered and staying at the Meadowville Hilton. The desk clerk knew her. A bartender named Pete Burger knew her.

She carried identification in the name of Dina Forrest, and traveler's checks made out in that name. When she didn't immediately regain consciousness, the police tried to locate next of kin. They'd been unsuccessful so far. There was no phone at the address in her identification. They'd written, but the letter had come back marked "not at." They'd assumed her memory wouldn't be permanently impaired, so they hadn't pushed it.

But what had happened to her? It looked like an attempted mugging that had been interrupted, though things like that hardly ever happened in Meadowville. But the times were bad, and no place was really safe. She was told that a man named Red Stanton had been going to his pickup truck in the Hilton parking lot. He'd stumbled over her, called an ambulance, gone with her to the hospital. The emergency room had made a report to the police. They'd looked around, but hadn't found anything. Pete Burger had confirmed that she'd had a drink in the Hide-away only half an hour before she was found. She was a lucky girl that it hadn't been worse. At least she was alive . . .

Five days later she was released from the hospital. She still didn't know who she was, or why she'd come to Meadowville. Or if she was on her way somewhere for a reason, and where that somewhere was, or why she was going. In fact, she still felt like a newborn child. She just didn't know anything. Except that she was a grown woman and, according to her identification, she was originally from New York City, at a certain address, and was twenty-six years old, with a name that meant nothing to her.

When she paid her bill at the hospital with the traveler's checks, she was left with two hundred dollars. She went back to the Hilton again because she didn't know where else to go, and because she wanted to rest and think about what had happened to her, think about what she should do. Although she didn't admit it to anyone else, she was scared.

The doctor had suggested she go back to New York, telling her that familiar surroundings might bring her memory back. She was afraid to and she didn't know why. She could imagine herself knocking at a door and asking and somebody saying they didn't know her face, hadn't ever heard of Dina Forrest. She could imagine another dead end.

The police had shown her dozens of pictures of men and boys. She guessed they were of people who had records for mugging. Nobody looked familiar to her. Nobody reminded her of anyone she'd ever seen. She guessed from the way the police acted that that was just what they expected. Beyond that, they didn't have anything to offer. But they, like the doctor, told her not to worry. It would work itself out. One morning she'd wake up and it would all have come back to her.

She didn't believe them. All she knew was the fact of her

own terror. Plainly the only response that was smart was to stand still and wait, she thought, and that was what she decided to do.

The desk clerk welcomed her, gave her the key to her room. She found her way without any trouble, and was pleased that she remembered that much. Maybe it was a sign.

But she had a new shock when she looked at her belongings. She could have sworn on a stack of Bibles that none of them had ever belonged to her. Dull. That was the word for the shirts and skirts that hung in the closet. And the shoes . . . ugh! Low-heeled, blacks and browns. It was the same with her makeup, what there was of it. What kind of stuff was that? And her hair, when she looked in the mirror, disgusted her. Hanging on her shoulders like a dish mop. A flat blond, washed out. Dull. God, what a mess. What the hell had she been thinking of?

She swung away from the mirror. There were going to be some changes made, she thought, and fast. That was all there was to it. She wasn't going to go on looking like that. Never mind if this was how she'd always looked before. She didn't remember it so it didn't matter. Now was different. And she'd be different, too.

She counted her money. Forty-five dollars. Eighty-seven cents in change. Two hundred dollars in unused traveler's checks. And she owed the hotel bill. She sank down on the edge of the bed.

She'd have to do something. And quick.

One thing she was sure of. She couldn't sit around and wait to remember who she was or what she was doing in Meadowville. If it came to her sometime, then fine. But if not . . . she fought back a sudden surge of fear . . . if not, then so what? What did it really matter?

She knew who she was now. Dina Forrest. Starting from scratch. Suddenly she heard herself laugh aloud. The sound surprised her. The feeling surprised her, too. It felt good to laugh. Oh, yes, it really felt good.

She got up, danced a few steps, watching her legs in the mirror. They were nice legs, and the ache was gone. The dancing felt good

But when she looked at the rest of herself, her spirits sagged. God, what a mess.

She grabbed lipstick, and colored her mouth. The shade was wrong, but it would have to do for now. No eye makeup. Hell. No rouge. Oh, for Pete's sake. Well, she'd do the best she could with what she had. And right now, as soon as she was cleaned up again and dressed. Never mind the money. She was going to go out and get what she wanted.

When she started to change, she frowned. What was she wearing that stupid bra for? She didn't need it. Her breasts were full but high and firm. She looked better without all that strapping in. Even in that dumb suit jacket.

A few minutes later, she was on her way to the drugstore. She didn't have to think about finding her way.

She knew exactly where it was and how to get there. Two blocks along Century Boulevard. A turn left into Greene Street, and down the mall right to the end. It occurred to her as she went in the door that she must have been there before . . .

She gathered twenty dollars worth of makeup and took it to the cashier, impatient with anticipation. She could almost see how she'd look. Lashes darkened. Eyelids shadowed. Color in her cheeks. A pink glow that that would highlight her face. But as the clerk checked the items, Dina grew more and more uneasy. Finally she blurted, "No, never mind. I've got to think about it," and rushed out of doors. She stopped, squinting through tears into bright sunshine. She felt as if she had walked into a brick wall. Her feet wouldn't go forward any more. The breath went out of her as if she'd been hit hard between her shoulders. Damn it! What was the matter with her? She wanted that makeup. What was she doing out here, empty handed? She swung around, chin tilted defiantly. She went back into the drugstore. Without apology, she told the clerk to ring up the purchases. Her arms full, she walked out. That was better. It was right. Happily, she went into a shop. She spent three-quarters of an hour trying on blouses before she finally settled on a low-cut green one. She didn't think it was the best color in the world for her. It didn't look right with her hair. But she wanted it, and wanted it so much, that she took it anyway.

As soon as she got back to the hotel, she redid her face. Then she put on the blouse with a flared white skirt. For an instant, she stared at herself. The blood drained from her face. Dizziness swept her. What was she doing? Who was she? She looked so strange to herself. So . . . cheap, maybe. Flashy. It just wasn't right . . .

Then her head cleared. Her reflection brightened and shone. Twirling in front of the mirror, she laughed again. That was right. That was more like it. Except damn it, she just didn't like her hair . . .

By then it was late afternoon. She wanted a drink. She went down to the Hide-away. The bartender said, "Terrible thing that happened to you. I'm glad you're okay now."

She grinned at him. "Me too," she said, and leaned forward so that he could see down her blouse.

He took a step back, surprised. That sure wasn't like her, he later told his wife.

"You know," Dina said. "I kind of like this town. So I'm going to stay."

"That right? You told me you were pushing on to San Francisco."

"I did?" She laughed. "Oh, well, I've changed my mind. Of course I'm going to have to get a job. So if you hear anything, then let me know."

That surprised him, too. She was so . . . well, he didn't quite know how to say it, he told his wife. It was how she said it, kind of forward. Hinting at he didn't know what. And whatever it was, he wasn't sure he liked it.

But he said, "Sure. If I hear of anything I will. Want the usual?" At her nod, he got her a rum and Coke.

She took a sip, put it down, shaking her head. "Too sweet. I hate Coke. How about a Scotch on the rocks?"

That was Pete Burger's third surprise. But he got her another drink anyway, and watched her taste it.

Just then Red Stanton climbed on the bar stool beside her.

Pete gave Red a beer and went away to serve someone else. When he looked back, Red was laughing over at her and she was leaning close to Red, and Pete wondered what they were saying to each other.

What Pete couldn't hear was Red introducing himself, adding, "I'm glad you're okay. I thought you were dead when I first found you."

"So you're the one," she said, her eyes bright. "If you hadn't come along then I would have been dead, I think."

He shrugged. "Somebody else would have found you pretty soon."

"I'm very grateful." The words were prim, but the tone wasn't.

Red's shoulders braced. He snapped his fingers at Pete. "One more for the lady."

"Why, thank you," she said. She was being demure, but not quite.

Red told her she was lucky she'd recovered and she agreed. He asked if she knew what had happened, who had hit her and why. She explained that she had no idea. Then he asked her plans, and she said she was looking for a job.

"You are? How come?"

"I like Meadowville," she told him. "I feel I belong here, so I want to stay. And to do that I'll need an income." It felt good to hear the words aloud again. It confirmed her decision. She found herself laughing.

Red knew that June was expecting him home for a late dinner. But that didn't stop him. He leaned close to Dina. "Listen, would you like to have something to eat?"

"I'm starving," she said. "Really, I'm starving."

He stared at her for a second, surprised and shaken. It was almost as if he was hearing an echo. Something he'd heard before. Something he'd heard a long time ago . . . But then his grin slanted sideways. He dropped bills on the bar for Pete, adding a larger-than-usual tip. "Come on. Let's get you fed, and talk about that job you want."

The next day Red was supposed to be at Claude's finishing up the job. He'd said it would take maybe a week, but he hadn't

150

been in any hurry to finish it so, although there were only some small details to take care of, he had let it drag on. Instead of going to work, Red had met Dina. They'd had coffee together, then he'd taken her to see Willie Harker.

Willie looked her over, rubbing the bristles on his jaw. "Sure. I'll take you on. I need somebody to answer the phone in the office. Do my letters. You can type, can't you? Help me with the contracts."

The pay wasn't much, but all right. The hours, nine to five, were good. Dina agreed to start the next morning. There wasn't any reason to wait.

When they left Willie's used-car lot, she said, "You're acting like a Chinaman, Red."

"What?" He had a quick, pained memory of small slant-eyed men scrambling from a dugout amid leaping flame.

"That's what they say. When a man saves your life, then he's responsible for you forever. And that's how you're acting. First you saved my life and now you've gotten me a job."

He smiled down at her. "Is that bad?"

"Oh, no," she laughed. "I like being taken care of."

And he was a big taker-care-of. That's how he'd gotten tangled up with June. He thought of that, then shrugged So what? Dina Forrest was sure no June.

"Let's see about getting you a room," he said. "The Hilton's too high to stay in for good. You're going to need somewhere better to lay your pretty head."

She said she'd better wait until she saw how the job worked out, and told him she wanted to go shopping. He dropped her off at the Century Mall, promising to return for her in two hours.

She spent the two hours buying. A brown stuffed teddy bear.

151

A frilly nightgown and robe to match. High-heeled sandals. She had very little money left by the time Red came back for her. But it didn't matter. She wasn't worried about it. She had a job, and she'd earn more. And if worse came to worse, she could maybe borrow a fifty or so from Red Stanton.

The following day she discovered that sometime, in her other life, the life she no longer remembered and hardly felt that she had lived, she must have known how to type. When she sat down her hands flipped over the keyboard as if they'd been at it for years. She felt she'd been there forever by the time Red appeared to take her to lunch at the noon break.

It was as if it was something she'd done before. The typing. Answering the phone. Walking down the street with Red.

For a little while she puzzled over it. She had the feeling she was mixed up, but she didn't know what she was mixed up about. It was familiar, but confused. Finally she let it go. She knew she had to expect funny feelings. It came with the loss of memory. With starting over from scratch as if she were newborn. Naturally she'd get funny feelings once in a while. Who wouldn't under those circumstances? But she wasn't going to worry about it.

If her past came back, well, it would be okay. Good even. She'd know who Dina Forrest was, where she'd been, where she was going when she came to Meadowville. If it didn't, well that was all right too. She was still somebody, still her own person. And going by what that first Dina Forrest had owned, the new one was much more pleasing. Those ugly clothes . . . that drab makeup. Even sweet rum and Coke for drinks. Ugh! Scotch on the rocks was better. Now if only she could figure out what to do with her hair. . . .

Red wanted to meet her for dinner that night. But she said

no. She wanted to take it easy and rest. She'd curl up and watch television and get a good sleep.

He was more disappointed than he expected to be, but he accepted the answer. There was plenty of time. He finished up at Claude's late that afternoon, and then went home and got drunk.

When June said something to him, something he didn't even hear, he reared back and slapped her. She stared at him, her blank eyes wide and her mouth turned down. He couldn't stand looking at her, so he stamped out.

He went to the Hide-away but Dina wasn't there, and hadn't been, according to Pete Burger. Red spent the rest of the evening telling Pete that married life was hell. A man was born to be free. And ought to be. It was his God-given right.

While he went on about that, his mind was ranging away. He was thinking about Dina, wanting her, and damning himself for having gotten himself trapped by June.

CHAPTER 12

Liz hesitated on the threshold of the front room. It was almost as if she felt the presence of something blocking her way. An invisible wall. A barrier she could sense but not see. Finally she took a deep breath and went in.

The padded wheelchair stood near the window, empty now. The bed was made up, covered with a blue and white checked quilt.

Liz picked up the silver bell that stood on the bedside table. It felt cold to the touch. As cold as her mother's face had felt when Liz found her a little more than three weeks before. Then it had been early October, with brilliant sun and the trees draped in red and gold. Now the days were gray, the maples bare. The shops were full of the orange and black paraphernalia of Halloween.

There had been a time when her mother had made costumes. A pirate outfit for Liz. A gypsy dress for Maggie. They'd baked cookies and lit candles for jack-o'-lanterns.

Now Maggie was gone. And her mother too. Liz stood very

still, trying to recall the blurred passage of recent days.

There had been a lot to do. Plans to make. Questions to answer. Calls on her for which she had somehow managed to summon a strength she didn't think she had.

"It had been coming for a long time," Dr. Detrick told her. "I've been preparing you for years. So you must have realized . . ."

She said nothing then. But later, when they were alone, she told Richard what she was thinking. "I oughtn't to have left her that night."

"It wouldn't have made any difference."

She could tell that he was worried about her. He sensed that she wasn't saying everything that she felt.

And she knew she had to. "You remember, Richard. Claude was there that day. I told you about his visit. It was such a peculiar coincidence. The way he turned up. Just after she'd been talking about inviting him for dinner. I tried to talk her out of it of course, and the next thing I knew he was there, ringing the doorbell."

Richard's face had hardened. His gray eyes flashed. "For God's sake, Liz!"

"I didn't want to hear them talk, you see, didn't want to be part of it. So I ducked out and left mom alone with him. I went into the kitchen to make tea, and fiddled with a shopping list."

"Part of what?" Richard had asked.

"I knew what it would be. What they'd talk about. A rehash of the past. Of Maggie. And how it was. As mom thought it. And how it was, as Claude said. And I just didn't want to hear it, so I left them alone together."

"You know she was all right later on. The talk couldn't have hurt her."

155

"He was there, Richard. It had to do with him." Her voice had dropped. "It's what I was afraid of from the beginning. From when you first told me he was coming back to town."

Richard had put a hand under her chin, tilted her face up. "Liz, are you blaming me?"

"No. Of course not." But there had been uncertainty in her voice. She didn't know. She wasn't sure. But if Claude hadn't come back . . .

"Liz," Richard had said. "Oh, Liz. He held her tight against him, pressing his lips to her hair. "Don't. Don't spoil it for us."

"I'm not," she'd answered, drawing away. "It's just that . . . I can't help it. Claude scares me. I guess he always has. That's what Maggie said, too."

"You're not being reasonable," Richard protested.

"She *did* say it," Liz had cried. "I can remember how it was. I think it was the night before it happened. Anyway, his father was already dead. And she said you could never tell what Claude would do. Maybe he didn't even know himself. Maybe he couldn't help it. But you couldn't ever be sure of him. I asked her why she kept seeing him. And she said, 'Why not?' and laughed. And then she said it was fun not knowing for sure."

. . . Maggie sitting cross-legged on her bed. A shoe on the windowsill. Its mate on the chair, buried by a slip, a pair of panties and three used tissues . . .

"She was a child," Richard had said. "Seventeen. A child talking the way kids do."

Liz had shaken her head. "You never knew Maggie as I did. I suppose nobody could. She was sweet, and very grown up in a lot of ways. But there was more to her than that. There was

156

a kind of risk-taking side to her . . . a need to challenge and tempt . . . sometimes it made her seem more than grown up. Made her seem . . . old."

"You were so young yourself, Liz."

Shivering, she'd said softly, "I'm so mixed up."

He drew her back into his arms. "Of course you are. There've been so many changes. You've had a lot of responsibility for a long time, and now you're on your own. But I want you to start thinking about us. It's time. I've been waiting. But enough's enough."

"I can't. Not yet."

"Why not?"

"I don't know." She buried her face in his shoulder. "I just can't."

"And you won't talk about it either," he'd said softly.

"There's nothing . . . at least not yet . . . I need time."

"All right," he'd said. "All right, Liz."

But she'd seen the look on his face. She knew she didn't have much time. . . .

And yet she couldn't think about getting married. Not so soon. She looked at the empty padded wheelchair. At the silver bell she still held in her fingers.

Something had happened. Either when Claude was here with her mother, or later, when Liz was with Richard. Whenever it had been, Liz should have been there. To protect her mother. But from what? she asked herself.

Slowly Liz backed out of the room.

Claude had gone to the store for eggs, but seeing the Halloween candy he stopped to buy three full bags. He was sure that the kids were still going for "tricks or treats" after dark on Halloween night. Nothing had changed in Meadowville. Certainly not that, he thought.

When he got home he settled down to work, leaning over the drawing board as he always did. The pencil felt peculiar in his fingers. More like a weapon than a tool to which he had been long accustomed. He drew a single line and it ripped through the paper. He tore off the page and began another. The pencil still felt strange to him. He threw it down. He turned on the radio, listened while a quiet monotone said that hard-liners in the Iranian parliament had prevented a quorum. Which meant that the hostage issue wouldn't be discussed that day. He growled to himself, cut the radio off and turned on the fluorescent gooseneck lamp that hung over his shoulder. Light flooded the paper. He took up the pencil again.

The house creaked and sighed. A cold breeze blew on his back from the big window that Red had put in for him. The mockingbirds cheeped in the eaves.

It was quiet. Too quiet. He was accustomed to hammering, banging, the whir of the saw. He was used to swearing and conversation.

But what conversation? He shouldn't miss that. Not after what he'd heard. Red and his big mouth. Red, not caring what he said, maybe even hoping to be overheard. Claude's stomach turned over at the memory.

He bent his head, gripped the pencil, forced himself back to work. The lines slowly began to appear. He forgot his thoughts, forgot everything except what was coming out of the pencil onto the drawing paper. The good time. Medicine for what ailed him. Work.

Hours later, he sat back, smiling. He had one more strip

finished. He'd thought he could work here, anywhere. But there'd been a small, niggling doubt. Now he was sure it would be okay.

He got up, stretched. He was hungry, thirsty. But first . . . He packed the drawing between cardboard, made up the label. Tomorrow he'd go to the post office.

The Halloween candy remained undisturbed on the tray near the door.

He'd heard cars outside and the sound of giggling. No one had knocked at the door. When the late news was over, he gave up and went to bed.

Sometime later he was awakened. Tires squealing. Muffled voices. He waited, but nothing happened. In a little while he fell asleep again.

It was a gray morning, and raining. He fixed his usual big breakfast while listening to the early news. It didn't look as if the hostages would be freed before the election four days away. There was disagreement about how that would affect the outcome. He turned the radio off, drank his third cup of coffee to the sound of rain on the window.

Taking the wrapped drawing with him he went outside. Sodden leaves made a slippery carpet underfoot. The cold air knifed through his jacket, but he hardly noticed it.

He looked across the front yard, at first unable to understand what he saw. It looked like a row of shiny gray robots spaced feet apart. Then they became upended garbage cans. A row of emptied cans, standing in the refuse with which they had been filled. There was a stench in the air. Broken bottles gleamed amid aluminum foil. A few orange and black streamers hung over the mess as an obscene decoration.

Sickened, he backed away. He put the drawing aside and leaned against the door, his long body shaking.

He had to do something. But what? *What?*

He remembered the sound of car tires squealing, the voices. It hadn't been kids. They couldn't have managed so many garbage cans. What should he do? Claude asked himself again.

He went inside, intending to phone, then stopped. The police. Loud, questioning voices. Hard, staring eyes. No. He couldn't stand that.

He went to the door and looked out. Of course the cans were still there. Why had he hoped otherwise? He had to do something. After a while he got a shovel from the garage and cleaned up the mess. He filled the cans, set them in a neat row along the curb.

He started out again after scrubbing his hands. It was still very cold. He decided it was time to get out a heavy overcoat. But it was all right for now. Mostly he'd be in the car.

But the starter whined, didn't catch. He stamped it again, twisted the key. Another whine. Damn Willie Harker. Damn all used cars. Claude waited, tried again. Still no good.

He got out, taking the package with him. Though it was bulky and hard to handle, he could manage. He walked the seven blocks through the rain to the post office.

By then he was soaked through. Hair plastered to his head. Face wet. His glasses immediately fogged over when he got inside. Stumbling, he made his way to the counter.

Red Stanton was talking to the clerk, a small, rabbity-looking man. Red grinned at Claude, took his time before finishing the conversation. "Okay, Bubba, I'll see you," he said finally, and turned away.

The clerk gave Claude a peculiar look. "In case you didn't

notice, it's raining out there."

"I did notice," Claude said.

"You want this insured?"

Claude said yes, named the amount, added that he wanted the package registered, return receipt requested.

"Monetary value?" the clerk asked.

"None."

"Then what's it all about?"

When Claude didn't answer, the clerk shrugged and turned away. But as Claude went to the door, the clerk said, "The man's crazy. He insured something with no monetary value. Wanders around in the pouring rain. And that look he just gave me . . ."

Claude hurried outside. Crazy. To hell with him. But that didn't erase the words. They kept echoing in his mind. It's what the police would have said if he'd called them about the garbage. They'd probably think he'd done it himself. Collected those cans and dumped them in his own front yard.

He turned down Main Street, heading toward Willie Harker's. They'd have to do something. Send a tow truck. Pull the car in so the mechanic could look at it. If they couldn't do anything right away, Willie would have to make it good. Claude would see that he did.

From the corner of his eye he saw a red umbrella across the street. He turned to look. A red umbrella. A very short black shiny raincoat flaring over slender legs. A quick, saucy bouncing walk. Something . . . he didn't know what exactly . . . just a sweet familiarity about the movement, the form, locked him in place. His rain-wet face was suddenly wet with fresh tears. Oh, God, God . . . it wasn't possible. It wasn't. It couldn't be.

He plunged toward the street as a truck barreled by, and he

leaped back just in time to save himself. A sheet of filthy water whipped him. A horn blared. A curse trailed back. Panting, he crossed over, but the red umbrella was gone.

He walked two blocks one way, then retraced his steps and went two blocks in the opposite direction.

Two girls, hurrying, their heads wrapped in plastic scarves. A young boy hugging a dog in his arms. A fat woman trudging along in cracked shoes.

It was no good. No red umbrella. No small, slim form. But she was here. Somewhere. She was. He'd seen her. He couldn't be wrong.

Slowly, hands in his pockets, not noticing the rain, he headed for Willie's. But his mind was full of what he'd seen. A girl carrying a red umbrella. So what? But that walk, saucy, quick, bouncy . . . Almost a dance . . . Maggie . . .

No. It was impossible, he reminded himself.

He managed to tell Willie about the trouble with the Volare, received an apology, a promise that a truck would go out. The mechanic would either fix it on the spot or bring it in. Either way Claude didn't have to worry. Willie Harker always took care of his customers. Claude knew that, didn't he?

"Looked like a madman," Willie later told Vernon Meese. "I never saw anything like it. Wild-eyed. Hair soaked. Jacket too. I tell you I began to feel sorry for that boy. And what I'd really like to do is run him out of town."

Vernon nodded over his coffee cup, thinking of oranges spinning out of his hands. Only a few days before, he'd been talking to Red and had mentioned the recreation center again. And only a little while ago he'd heard in the Depot Cafe that somebody driving down Vickery Street had seen a mess of garbage on Claude's front lawn, and Claude ankle deep in it, shoveling and cursing. A very unstable person, Claude Vickery, Vernon thought. You never knew what would happen to him. Vernon wondered who had helped Red. Or if he'd managed alone.

Finally Vernon told Willie that he understood how Willie felt, but that Claude still had a long way to go.

Claude didn't know what the others were saying. He only knew what he was feeling. He'd forgotten that he'd spent two hours cleaning up garbage. He covered all of Main Street on foot, then walked out to the Century Mall and back. His head tilted forward, his shoulders slouched, hands in his pockets, he peered into every face he passed. Looking for the sweet familiarity . . .

Sometime, he wasn't sure when, he began to wonder if maybe he'd seen Liz Paige. Liz, walking with a red umbrella. Liz was taller than Maggie had been . . . But maybe, from that distance, and in the rain . . .

It was late afternoon when he reached her house. The shadow of Dead Man's Bluff had already fallen across the town. He rang the doorbell.

When she opened the door, he realized that he oughtn't to have come. Hope died in him. There was no sweet familiarity. Nothing to remind him of Maggie.

Liz's face was cold and unwelcoming. He felt chill emanate from her in an icy current. He didn't know why. He'd never done anything to her. Never. Nothing. There'd been the accident with Maggie. But that's what it had been. An accident. Everybody knew that. Nobody could blame him. And he'd paid, hadn't he? . . . The red umbrella . . . the girl dancing along the street . . . No. It couldn't have been Liz.

He had to say something. He blurted, "Liz, I'm sorry about your mother."

"I know, Claude. You told me. At the funeral."

He remembered looking at Maggie's grave. She had been there, under the earth. Hadn't she? Wasn't she still?

He was obviously shivering. His teeth chattered between blue lips. But Liz didn't invite him in.

"Your mother seemed so good that day we were talking. Bright. And cheerful. And . . . and . . ." The words faded under the weight of her hot blue stare. He'd wanted to say that they'd only talked about Maggie. But he couldn't. He drew a deep breath. "Well, I just wanted to say I'm sorry about what happened. And I wanted to tell you she was feeling good, and happy."

"Thank you," Liz said.

Then, to his utter surprise, he blurted, "It's funny. But you don't look a bit like Maggie, do you?"

Liz winced, said nothing.

"And you don't own a red umbrella, do you?"

She shook her head.

He forced a smile. "It must have been somebody else. It's just that I saw . . . I thought maybe it was you . . ."

"I'm sorry, Claude. I have to go. There's something on the stove."

"Oh, sure. I'm sorry I bothered you. But thanks, thanks."

The door snapped shut in his face before he had finished speaking. He turned away quickly, telling himself that he'd better not go to the Paige house any more. Ellen Paige was gone. Liz didn't want to see him. So that was that. He just wouldn't go there any more.

He walked back to Harker's. The used-car lot was closed, but his Volare was waiting for him. He got in, drove home. And all the way he looked for a girl carrying a red umbrella.

That night he saw the headlights creep along the road ahead of him as he drove up Dead Man's Bluff. He felt Maggie's hand burning on his thigh. He awakened, sweating, to the sound of the garbage truck grinding in the street below, and the crashing of six empty cans on the sidewalk.

While he was shaving he began to think of how plain and bare Maggie's grave had been. No flowers there. No gold chrysanthemums to warm the cold earth. There had been white wreaths for Ellen Paige, but none to warm the earth where Maggie lay. He told himself it didn't matter. But when he'd had coffee, he drove out Century Boulevard and bought a huge bouquet. A little later he stood at Maggie's graveside, clasping the flowers to his chest.

But he found himself thinking of Liz. It was nagging at him, pushing him. Why had she acted so funny the day before? What did she have against him? What was wrong?

Though he knew he shouldn't be there, a little later he was at Liz's door, still clutching the flowers to his chest.

He rang the doorbell and waited. There was no answer. He rang it again and again. But Liz didn't come.

He threw the flowers in the back of the car and got in and sat looking up at the house past the unkempt front lawn to the window from which Ellen Paige used to watch the street, looking for Maggie.

He could hear Ellen's voice in his mind. *Now you're here, Claude . . . I'm sure, so sure of it. I know Maggie'll come back. No matter what anybody says. She loved you, Claude. And you loved her. So now she'll come back . . .*

He shivered, thinking of it. Because he'd known as she spoke that Ellen Paige had lost her mind. At first he'd thought it was a manner of speaking when she said that Maggie was close by. That she'd almost seen Maggie walk with him up the path to the house. But soon he realized what she meant. And he knew Maggie was dead. And yet . . . The older woman had been so certain.

He leaned forward suddenly. Something moved at the front window. Maggie! he thought. Maggie . . .

He wanted to get out of the car, but couldn't. He wanted to drive away. But he was frozen in place. Frightened by what he'd seen, by his own thoughts. Maggie.

In a little while reason returned. He knew he'd seen Liz at the window. Liz, looking at him, then turning away.

And inside the house, Liz wept into the phone, saying, "Richard, I just can't stand it. He was here yesterday, and saying the most stupid things to me. And he's come back today. With flowers. Flowers, Richard. And when I wouldn't open the door, he went and sat in his car. He's still there. Yes. He's there right now. Just sitting and staring at the house."

"Calm down," Richard told her. "I'll be right over."

"And then . . ."

"I'll be there."

But by the time he arrived, Claude had gone.

"You have to tell him to stay away from me," Liz said immediately.

She was pale, her eyes shadowed, a new thinness in her cheeks.

"I'll go over tonight," Richard agreed.

"And tell him straight out. I'd do it myself, but you'll be better, kinder, than I could."

"Okay," Richard said. But he knew he wouldn't be able to do it. Not straight out. And Liz would get over it. Whatever it was. She'd damn well have to.

"If you just say it upsets me to see him . . ."

Richard nodded. "I'll figure it out." But he could see that she was already beginning to regret her outburst.

"It's just that he keeps looking at me," she said hesitantly. "When he sees me he stares so. As if he expects something."

"Liz, please stop this."

"Expects something," she repeated. "And I don't know what it is." But she thought she knew. And it frightened her.

Claude wanted her to turn into Maggie.

And she couldn't, didn't even want to. Although she remembered when she had wished she could. Seventeen-year-old Maggie . . . going off to her part-time summer job in their father's office . . . grown up enough to type and file and answer the phone . . . Coming home, arms laden with packages, makeup, clothes . . . and gaily dressing for the boys who always surrounded her. While fifteen-year-old Liz did household chores and wore jeans and sneakers and listened to stories about the boys. She couldn't be Maggie then, though she had longed to. And she couldn't be Maggie now.

"Look," Richard was saying. "You're imagining it. He's lonely. He needs friends. He feels that the town is against him."

"I'm just saying what he does, Richard."

"Forget about him. And think about me."

"I can't," she whispered. "Don't you see? It's all mixed up together."

He wanted to shake her. She was making complications where there weren't any. It was so simple to him. There was nothing to keep them apart now. All they had to do was get married. He fought back his impatience. "Okay, you're mixed up. Now what are you driving at?"

"Claude . . ."

"Jesus!" Richard exploded. "Forget Claude, will you?"

"Mom was okay until he came back."

"Liz! You knew all along something had to happen."

"But the things I think . . . and I can't help it . . ."

"You sit around, brooding. You've got to get busy instead of this piddling around in the past. Your mother. Maggie. What your mother said about Maggie. None of it makes sense. And you know it." He went on briskly, "Now get out of those jeans and into something else. Do up your face, or whatever. We're going to have dinner out, and go dancing at the Hideaway."

"Richard, I can't do that. It's too soon. Maybe just dinner . . ."

"Dinner and dancing," he said firmly.

She gave in, but with little enthusiasm. And upstairs, while she was dressing, she remembered that Claude had spoken about a red umbrella. Somebody carrying a red umbrella. Like the one that Maggie had had. Liz distinctly remembered it. Red, with a black handle. When Maggie got it one Christmas she immediately began to pray for rain so she could use it. She ended up using it when there was no rain.

Liz didn't mention that to Richard.

They had a good evening together and, later, an even better night in each other's arms. When he left her in the morning, he kissed her, hugged her close to him. "Start thinking about the date," he said. "It's time we got married. Okay?"

She promised she would. But as soon as he was gone she

went into the front room. It seemed to her that she could smell her mother's scent. A sweet dry odor. It seemed to her that she could see her mother sitting in the wheelchair near the window. Her mother's voice seemed to be echoing in the silence.

Liz picked up the silver bell, rang it as hard as she could. It made a soft tinkle.

She looked at the chair again, raised her head to listen. Maybe that's what her mother had meant. Saying Maggie was so near. Maybe her mother hadn't been crazy. Maybe that was it—or was it?

Liz burst into tears and ran from the room. Maybe she was going crazy, too.

"Used his yard for a garbage dump," June was saying. "Red said he heard it in town."

It gave Richard the excuse he needed. He called Claude, asked how he was, said he'd heard about the Halloween thing.

Claude said he was okay. He said he had cleaned up the mess, and then changed the subject. Richard told him that Liz said he'd been there but that she hadn't wanted to answer the door. "She's skittish just now," Richard explained. "She'll get over it."

"Sure," Claude agreed. "I understand. I shouldn't have gone there."

"She'll get over it," Richard repeated. When he hung up, he saw June standing in the doorway and realized she'd been listening to every word he said.

CHAPTER 13

Pete Burger served drinks over the bar, one eye on his customers, the other on Dina Forrest.

He heard half a dozen conversations at once. The election just over with Reagan winning. Big changes coming. And what about the hostages? Would they be coming home soon? He heard and tuned it all out. He'd heard most of it before. He wished he knew what Dina Forrest was saying to Red Stanton. Wishing didn't do any good. He got busy. The next time he looked, Dina was sitting up at the bar in her usual place, and Red was stamping out the door.

Dina grinned at Pete. She was feeling good. She'd made Red mad, but so what? That didn't matter. He'd come back. He was crazy about her, and she didn't care. He was married for one thing. For another what did he have to offer? There were plenty of other guys around.

She asked Pete for a Scotch on the rocks. When he brought it to her, she sipped it slowly, looking around.

Her eyes met those of a tall man sitting alone under a plastic palm tree. He was slouched over so she could see only an angle of his jaw and the glint of light on his glasses. Her gaze passed on, then swung back to him.

She didn't know why. It just happened. She just had to look back at him. As if it were supposed to happen. And suddenly she smiled. She couldn't help herself. If she had tried to stop, she wouldn't have been able to. She knew that. She didn't know why. She'd never seen the man before, and yet a smile bloomed on her lips. She raised her glass to him in a small salute. Even if she'd never seen him before, so what? This was 1980. And it was different now. But that didn't matter. She had always done what she wanted to anyhow.

He half-rose, then sank back, as if he didn't believe what he was seeing. As if he thought maybe his eyes were fooling him. Her smile grew wider. He looked as if he thought he were hallucinating.

Claude was gripped, struck by the sweet familiarity . . . A turn of the head that was the wrong color, but a turn that was so right. Narrow ankles in high-heeled sandals. The flashing smile. It was Maggie. Of course. It had to be. But no. It wasn't. The girl was a stranger. She couldn't be raising her glass to him. There had to be some mistake. But he knew there wasn't.

He could hear Ellen Paige speaking in his mind. *Now you're back, Claude, Maggie will come home too.* He banished the sound of her breathless words. It wasn't Maggie. Of course not. What was the matter with him? The only time he'd seen this girl before was when she was walking in the rain, carrying a red umbrella. But when his breath slowed and he knew he could move, he took off his glasses, slipped them into his breast pocket and went to the bar. He didn't speak to her. He was too shaky for that. But after he'd asked Pete for a drink and

171

gotten it, he sneaked a look in her direction.

She smiled at him again, patted the empty stool beside her.

He slid over, sat down. "For a minute I thought you were somebody else."

"You did?" Dina tossed her head. "I hope she's nice."

"She was very nice," Claude said solemnly. Was. He had to remember that. *Was.* He was listening as hard as he could, staring as hard as he could. The voice . . . no, not quite the same. But there was a certain inflection . . . The features . . . not much, not really. And yet . . . ? He stopped himself.

She gave her name, asked his.

"Oh, so you're Claude Vickery. I've heard about you. A friend of mine, Red Stanton . . ." She didn't say that Red had told her Claude was crazy as a hoot owl and belonged locked up where he couldn't do any more harm than he'd already done. She didn't mention that she'd understood the envy behind the remarks. What was Red Stanton against a Vickery, when measured in Meadowville? But it didn't matter to her. She liked Claude's looks. Not that he was handsome. But he had good eyes, warm and brown, and expressive. Now he was close, and not wearing his glasses, she could really see them. And he had a good nose and mouth, and a slow soft way of speaking that made him seem timid. But just the same there was something about him . . . she wasn't sure what it was. Maybe a hidden tension. Something afire inside of him. It was a little scary. Exciting almost. Like she couldn't be sure of which way he would jump if she pushed him. And there was all that property he was going to get. The house Red wanted for a recreation center for kids. She'd almost laughed when he told her about that. She was sure Claude Vickery had better sense than to give his house away for that. She decided

172

she wanted to know him and was going to make sure she would . . .

"Red?" Claude repeated. "Yeah, I know him."

He didn't sound overjoyed, but they went on talking. Dina told him about coming to in the hospital after the almost mugging and how Red had been the one who found her and took her there. Claude told her about returning to Meadowville from New York.

At that, she yawned, smiling still. "Me for bed, Claude."

He protested, but not too hard. He was tired too. He wanted to go home, to be alone to think. He wanted to sort out what he felt and what he feared.

Before they separated they made a date for the next evening.

While she was undressing in front of the mirror, she saw the brown teddy bear looking at her from the bed. Brown eyes. Brown eyes just like Claude's It was funny about that bear. Sometimes she slept cuddling it in her arms. Sometimes she threw it across the room before she climbed in.

She drew a brush through her hair, long, blonde. . . .

The next afternoon she took two hours off work. She went to a beauty parlor in the mall off Greene Street. Her appointment was for three-fifteen, and she was on time. But when she dropped into the chair, she was limp. She had started in, her hand on the door and then suddenly changed her mind. It was silly. She didn't need to do anything with her hair, she told herself. It had taken a long time to grow. Maybe she ought to think a little longer before deciding to cut it off. It was just plain silly. She was okay as she was. She didn't need to do anything with her hair. Except that even as she made the decision she felt as if she were going to explode right there in the mall off Greene Street. Her vision blurred, and her teeth

173

chattered. When she tried to turn away, her body shook and shuddered and her legs refused to obey her. The door opened, although she didn't feel as if she had pushed it. She stumbled through, as if she had been shoved from behind. Trembling, she waited her turn. And when her name was called, she followed the girl to a chair behind a pink curtain, and said in a shaking voice, what it was that she wanted.

She had her hair cut short and dyed a flaming red. She didn't know why. It was just a whim. A whim that had shaken her almost to pieces until she gave in to it. When the job was done, and she first looked at herself, a sweeping wave of nausea nearly drowned her. But it faded swiftly. She was left with strange mixed feelings. She loved it. She hated it.

It was like being divided in two.

She went back to work to finish a few small chores still a little sick to her stomach. Why had she cut her hair and dyed it? It didn't make sense. But it was all right. Somehow it just felt right. Somehow it even felt good.

She was better by the time she met Claude for dinner. Even though she'd just had a big fight with Red.

He'd called, said he wanted to see her. She told him no. She was busy. He said busy at what? So she told him. He growled, "If you're smart you'll stay away from Claude. He's nothing but bad news."

She told Red to mind his own business, and then he'd said he was coming over to talk to her. She told him, "Sure, I want to see you, Red. But not tonight. I don't belong to you, remember. I don't belong to anybody." The words felt good. They were familiar. She'd surely said them plenty of times before.

But Red didn't pay any attention. He asked about the next night and she agreed. They'd get together then. She hung up and forgot about him and dressed for Claude.

She wore a black see-through blouse and a full black skirt. It was maybe too dressy for where they would be going, she thought, but it didn't matter. She wore what she wanted to. When she wanted to. It was funny about the outfit though. It didn't feel as comfortable on her as she had thought it would when she picked it out.

She shrugged the thought away, pulled on a black velveteen coat and went down to wait for Claude.

He stopped just inside the lobby doors, frozen. Somebody came in behind him and bumped into him, thrusting him aside. He didn't notice, just stood there staring at her. She was sitting in a chair, her legs crossed, the black skirt pulled high. She held a cigarette somewhat clumsily, and stared at the smoke that drifted before her face. Her hair was a flaming red, curled, short. She was Maggie.

His heart gave a hitch in his chest. A long, icy shiver moved slowly from the top of his head to his toes. His throat closed tightly and his teeth clenched until the muscles in his jaws ached. Maggie. Oh, God, thank you. All he'd ever wanted. His Maggie. Come back for him.

But as he hurried toward her she got to her feet. And the sweet familiarity was gone. The reality of Maggie was gone. In spite of the red hair. In spite of the same shape and walk and smile. Maggie just wasn't there any more.

Sudden sweat broke out on his face. What the hell was happening to him? Maybe . . . maybe . . .

She put a hand on his arm. "Hi, didn't you recognize me?"

And suddenly it didn't matter. "You changed your hair, didn't you?"

She fluttered her fingers over the red curls. "Funny, hunh?

It just took me. A whim, I guess. So I went out had it done. You like?"

"Yes." His voice was intense. "Yes, I like it very much."

"Good." She grinned. But her expression was uncertain, and she touched the curls again. "It's funny. I'm just not sure."

"Be sure." He slid a hand under her elbow. "Would you like to go to the country club?" It didn't occur to him to wonder if they'd be admitted. The Vickerys had always belonged to the club.

"Wonderful." She beamed at him. "I've never been there before."

It was a new building. Fieldstone. Glass. Potted plants in the corners and in mid-room islands. More plants afloat from the ceiling. It had a new cool look to it that Dina didn't care for. Nothing homey and cozy. Holding hands in the place didn't seem to make sense to her.

Just the same, she and Claude held hands as they walked into the dining room.

Claude saw Liz and Richard right away. But he hesitated until Richard, after a whisper into Liz's ear, rose and waved.

Claude had wanted to be alone with Dina. At least that's what he'd thought. But coming to the club must have meant that he'd wanted something else, too. At least it seemed that way to him then. He felt good when he led Dina toward Liz and Richard, and introduced her to them, and accepted Richard's invitation to join them.

It was a rather stiff evening. Liz was very quiet. She greeted Dina, her blue eyes flickering over the flaming red hair. Then she sat back in her chair, barely touching her food. Richard was friendly, but he didn't seem to have much to say.

Claude managed to control his excitement. It was too soon

to let anybody guess. He wondered if Liz saw it, if Richard did. He couldn't tell.

Dina was bright, animated. She carried the conversation. She said to Liz, "You've lived in Meadowville all your life?" And: "It seems nice. That's why I stayed. But, oh, I don't know, sometimes I think I ought to go on. Only where?" And to Richard: "I'll bet you get to see lots of interesting things being a lawyer." And her eyes moved back and forth between Richard and Claude. It tickled her, being with the two men. She didn't know why. As for Liz . . . she was sweet, but she didn't matter. In a puzzling way Dina was very amused.

Claude was proud of her. While he ate two good-sized steaks and two baked potatoes, he sat smiling, doting on her with his eyes. It was the beginning for him and Dina.

For Liz and Richard it was the beginning of the end.

Later, driving home, she stared out of the window, hearing the faint murmur of Dina's voice in her mind. Trying to forget it. Trying not to think. But remembering anyway because she couldn't help it. Remembering how she'd felt when she first saw Dina's red hair. The shock. A cold stillness. Recognition. Then fear. What if . . .? Her mother's whispers suddenly loud. Just suppose . . . Could they still be sisters? And then remembering how Dina had insisted they go to the ladies room, confiding to her on the way, "I just wanted to talk to you a minute. I mean, by ourselves. Alone. To say I hope we're going to be friends."

Liz had forced herself to answer, "Of course." Her voice was steady, though she trembled inside. It scared her that she was at the same time drawn and repelled. She didn't want ever to see Dina Forrest again.

Dina giggled. "I guess you know all about me. As much as I know maybe. I mean, in this town, everybody knows everything, don't they?"

Liz had forced a smile to her lips.

"I feel better about it now," Dina went on. "Now that I'm making friends."

Liz had thought, *I'm not your friend. I can't be*. But she hadn't answered.

What if . . . ?

She didn't want to think about it any more. But she couldn't stop remembering.

Richard, silent until then, said, "I'm glad Claude's got somebody. That's what he needs."

"Somebody?"

"She seems like a nice girl."

Liz turned, looked at his profile. "Richard, didn't you notice?"

"Notice what?"

"The color of her hair." It was the obvious thing to mention, though there were other things as well.

"Sure," he said. "Plenty of people have red hair. So what?"

Liz was silent. Red hair. Like Maggie's. And the way she sometimes talked. Was she the girl carrying the red umbrella that Claude had seen? The red umbrella like one that Maggie had had?

Liz had promised herself that she'd never again tell Richard how often she found herself wondering if her mother could have been right. That Maggie could come back. She wouldn't let herself say that maybe, now, Maggie *had* come back. Maybe there was more to the whispering than anyone had understood.

178

Richard went on. "Yes, it's good. For Claude, I mean."

"Is it?" The question was quiet, despairing. How could it be good? If he was drawn to Dina because of the resemblance to Maggie, then he was kidding himself. If there was more . . . Liz wanted to scream. It couldn't be. It couldn't. What was she thinking? Why was she tormenting herself? She burst out, "Richard, why did you ask them to sit with us? You knew I didn't want you to. I'd told you before . . . Claude just . . . and that weird girl . . ." Her words, loud and heated, stopped her from remembering.

Richard looked surprised. "I asked you and you said it was okay."

"I was being polite. And you knew that, too." Too polite. It would have been better if she'd gotten up and walked away, left Richard with Dina and Claude. Better if she'd never tried to hide her shock at Dina's smile.

"Claude's a friend," Richard said, knowing that that wasn't going to be good enough. He went on. "I don't think it's good for him to be alone so much. That's what I meant when I said I was glad he had somebody. And that's why I wanted them to be with us. And be seen with us, too."

"There's something about her . . ." Liz began.

"It's the red hair. You think of Maggie."

"Yes," Liz agreed. Think of Maggie. Even feel Maggie. She didn't tell Richard that. And remember how Maggie had always said she could do anything, and had, because the rules were different for her. Liz didn't tell Richard that, either.

"She had long blond hair before," he said. "She's just dyed it."

Liz didn't answer.

"And she's nothing like your sister." Richard's voice was

firm. "Nothing like her. Really. Put it out of your mind. She had that accident or whatever it was, and is staying on. And she's good for Claude."

"I wonder."

"What do you mean by that?"

But Liz only shrugged. She didn't mention the color of Dina's hair any more. Or how her eyes blazed across the table at Claude, and then went swiftly to Richard's face.

"It'll be all right," Richard said. "It's got nothing to do with you. It's just this feeling you've got about Claude."

"You should have it too."

He sighed, didn't answer. It was useless. It worried him that she wouldn't listen to good sense. But she wouldn't. And he had to do what he thought was right.

"I mean it," she insisted.

"I know you do. But let's forget Claude for now. Okay?"

"And Dina too?"

"Yes," he said impatiently. "Now come on."

She stopped talking because there didn't seem to be anything to say. Richard wouldn't listen to her. He didn't understand.

It started out a bad day for Richard. He awakened late because he hadn't slept well. His night had been disturbed by dreams he no longer remembered, and didn't want to. He burned his tongue on stale coffee, charred the toast so that he couldn't eat it. When he went down to the office, June sat weeping over her typewriter.

She wouldn't say why. She wouldn't talk to him. She was afraid to say a word because if she did the whole thing would come out and she didn't want Richard to know about it.

Red had been both grouchy and drunk the night before. He'd demanded to know what Claude was up to. Was he visiting Richard often? Did they go out together? Had she heard anything about what happened on Halloween? What the hell was going on? And how come she wasn't telling him about it anyway? Dumb as she was, he had said, she must know how important it was. So she'd told Red she wasn't going to be a snitch any more. She was tired of it, tired of how he talked about Claude Vickery, who'd done nothing to Red, and nothing to anybody else either that she knew about. All he wanted was to live and get along like everybody else. That was when Red hit her. She told him she was tired of that, too. So he told her about Dina Forrest, and how pretty she was, and how he wanted her now and how he didn't want June.

And that was why June was crying. Because Red was all she had and, no matter what, she didn't want to lose him. When she wouldn't talk to him, Richard got her some of the stale coffee and retired to his office.

In quick succession came one blow after another.

First Willie Harker and Vernon Meese came to see him.

They'd talked it over the night before, after bringing it up with the Council of Aldermen and getting its approval. Vernon had been to Chicago to consult the Computo-Sales people. They'd be willing to wait six months. But not two years.

They laid it out on the table. Consider the jobs involved. The real estate. Consider what it would do for the town to have a brand-new clean industry moving in. Richard was counsel for the aldermen on a yearly retainer. It was a conflict of interest for him to represent Claude at the same time he worked for the council. When they were sure they had it worked out, they had two shots of bourbon apiece and talked it over again over a third one.

Now Vernon outlined the situation for Richard. Willie listened, nodding his dark head.

Richard's gray eyes began to harden. When Vernon finished presenting the case, Richard said coldly, "I don't see any conflict of interest. There's no litigation. It goes one way if Claude stays. It goes another if he leaves. And that's it."

"Right," Vernon agreed. "You go one way. Or you go the other. As far as we can see, you're going the other. Claude's hanging on because of you."

Richard pulled in a deep breath. The retainer was lost. He said, "Okay. I resign. Do you want it in writing."

"Not me," Vernon said hastily. "But the council . . . for its files . . ."

"I'm sorry," Willie told him getting to his feet.

"I am too," Vernon said.

"It's not going to change anything," Richard warned them. "You know that, don't you? You can't do a thing about John's will."

Vernon said only, "Well, we'll feel better about it, and that's something."

Hardly an hour later another client came by. He sat across from Richard, looking glum. "Understand you and Liz had dinner with Claude and some girl at the club last night."

Richard nodded, waited. He was beginning to get an idea of what was to come.

"It's just a matter of judgment," the client said. "You know. An attorney has to show a lot of it, doesn't he?"

"And what was bad judgment?" Richard demanded. "Taking my girl to the club? Running into an old friend?"

"An old friend from ten years ago."

"What did you want to see me about?" Richard asked, hoping to get it over with quickly.

"This business of John's will . . . Richard, it's given everybody in town a bad taste. They come into the store. They talk about it. And about Claude. And you, too."

"They're leaning on you to take your business elsewhere? Is that it?"

"They are. And the wife is, too."

Richard shrugged. "Okay. Thanks for telling me."

He knew now that he was right about the idea he had had.

A little later he received a call from the president of the Farmers and Mechanics Bank, asking that Richard come in to see him the following day.

"Is there a problem?" Richard asked.

"Not really," the man answered. "Just something I need to discuss with you."

"You've heard from the aldermen? From Vernon Meese. Is that it?"

"Yes," was the answer.

"Then let's save time," Richard said. "You feel the need to retain another attorney."

"That's about it," the man said.

"Okay," Richard agreed, and put down the phone.

Walter Cronkite was talking of the conditions just announced in Teheran for the release of the hostages. Liz only half-listened. He went on to talk about Reagan's transition team. She switched off the television set.

Richard picked up the conversation where it had stopped

183

when the news came on. "It's weird," he said. "They're against Claude, so they're pulling the ceiling down on me."

Liz rose, took a few aimless paces around the room, then sat on the sofa arm. Though the room was warm, she wore a heavy pink sweater and within it she shivered. She'd known Claude's return would mean trouble. She'd been right. And now there was Dina Forrest. The red hair so like Maggie's . . . the turn of the cheek . . . the bright eyes that flashed between Richard and Claude, flashed and lingered at the same time. It was impossible, of course. But Liz heard her mother's whispering again.

She ignored it, said quietly to Richard, "They're thinking birds of a feather. You're with them or against them."

"It's stupid. And unfair. ᴛᴏ me. And to Claude. What's he done to bring this on?"

"You know."

"That was a long time ago."

"People don't forget." She was speaking for herself as well as the others.

"It boils down to the estate," Richard said. "You can say what you think. I know it's just a matter of low-down, disgusting greed."

She fixed her blue eyes on the toes of her shoes. "Whatever, it's going to wreck you. And you don't deserve it."

"I won't let them club me, Liz." But he wasn't sure how he could stop them. If he lost all his clients, could he manage taking care of a few poor souls the court appointed him to represent? And maybe he wouldn't even get those.

Liz looked up at him, said softly, "Drop him, Richard. Stay away from him. It's not your fight. Maybe then it'll be okay."

"He's my friend," Richard protested. "I owe him. From

when I was a kid. That's got to mean something." Richard was thinking about the morning he first heard of the accident. Claude was in the hospital. Richard had wanted to go to him, had started out and then turned back, telling himself it wasn't the right time. He was thinking about when Claude had been taken to jail. He'd stayed away then, too. He remembered the letters he'd planned to write, the visits he'd thought to make, when Claude was sent away. He'd done neither.

Liz hadn't answered him, he suddenly realized. "Never mind Claude, he said. "Don't let this make a difference to us. Let's get married. And I mean right away."

"I want to," she said quietly. "I want to more than anything. But I can't. Not now, Richard."

He didn't ask her why. He thought he knew. She blamed him for bringing Claude home, blamed Claude for her mother's death, so that too came back to Richard himself. She was determined to punish him. And he wasn't going to let her.

Angry color flooded his face. He got to his feet, pulled on his coat, went to the door.

"Richard," she said quietly.

"I'll see you tomorrow," he answered.

When he left her, he stopped at Claude's. They spent the evening together in a bowling alley on Main Street. The game prevented much talk between the two men. It was just as well. Neither of them wanted conversation. Claude was preoccupied with thoughts of Dina. Richard was wondering what had happened to Liz.

CHAPTER 14

Left alone, Liz spent an hour fidgeting around the house. From the moment she first looked at Dina, Liz had heard her mother's whispering, *Maggie'll come back. I know.* The red hair. The sense of knowing, of recognition. The feeling of being at once drawn to and repelled by Dina. The impossibility seemed less certain than it ever had. What if . . . ?

Richard would say it was just Liz's imagination. And he had to be right. How could there be anything else? He would think of her mother maybe. As Liz was doing now.

Imagination. Or madness. Liz pressed her hands together. If she only knew. If only she could decide. Something was happening to her. But what?

Maybe, if she saw Dina alone for a little while, talked to her . . .

Liz acted on the thought as soon as it came to her. If she waited, weighed it, she wouldn't be able to do it. She pulled on her car coat, snatched up her purse and hurried outside.

She tried to plan what she would say on the ten-minute

drive. But when she tapped at Dina's door, and Dina opened it, her words were gone, the excuses forgotten.

Dina's hair, obviously just washed, and still dripping wet, looked very dark and straight. She was holding a towel, and wore a plain beige robe.

"Oh, Liz, hi. I was hoping you'd call me. Or stop by sometime. That's why I told you where I live. I'm sorry, I'm straight out of the shower. But come on in."

Liz went in, closed the door behind her. She didn't explain why she was there. Dina didn't seem to expect it.

"The place is a mess, but I'm not going to stay long. Only until I find a room that's cheaper."

Liz nodded, sat on a straight chair near the dresser. Dina was nothing like Maggie now. She was just a pretty girl, maybe a year or two older than Liz herself.

Toweling her hair, Dina giggled. "I don't know what got into me. I used to be a blond, you know. And then suddenly I got fed up with it and changed over." Her voice trailed away for a moment, then returned. "I'm still not sure I like it."

Liz said she thought it looked nice. It was common to try new hair colors nowadays. The conversation shifted to the town, Dina asking questions, Liz answering them, more and more reassured that Richard had been completely right. It was only the red hair that had gotten to Liz. There was nothing at all strange about Dina Forrest.

Suddenly Dina flung the towel aside, and a small grin touched her lips as she turned to the mirror. Speaking to it, watching Liz's reflected face, she said, "Claude told me that you and Richard are going together."

Liz nodded. "We have been for some time."

"When are you going to be married?"

"We haven't decided yet."

"You ought to do it soon," Dina told her. To Liz it somehow sounded like a warning. "Before something happens."

As Liz raised her eyes to stare at Dina she saw beyond the girl's shoulder to the windowsill. On it lay a single shoe. A slip hung on a lamp and, on the bed against the far wall, sat a chubby brown teddy bear.

Liz made no sound, though her throat tightened on a scream of terror. The bear was a twin to the one that Maggie had slept with for most of her life.

A bear like Maggie's . . .

Liz forced herself to look at Dina again. She had turned from the mirror, was watching Liz.

Liz waited until she was sure she could speak. "Is it true, really, that you don't know who you are?"

Dina nodded. "Just my name." But she didn't sound as if it mattered to her.

"Your name," Liz repeated, her voice more urgent. "And that's all?"

"Oh, I know I used to live in New York."

"Then how come you didn't go back? I'd have thought you'd try to find out . . ."

Dina shrugged. "I like it here. Maybe, one of these days, when I'm ready, I'll go and see what I can find out, but meanwhile, why bother? I know who I am now. And that's what counts."

"I suppose," Liz said dully. "Only, if it were me, I'd want to know, have to know."

Sudden sparks of malice glowed in Dina's eyes. "But you're not me."

Liz rose, looked at the teddy bear sitting on the stack of pillows. "No," she whispered through dry lips. "No. I'm not you."

With that, she turned and left, her footsteps echoing in the empty hallway.

CHAPTER 15

June pushed open the heavy glass door to Willie Harker's office. When it closed behind her, it seemed to sigh loudly, sounding just the way she felt. She looked the way she felt too. Her hair was tousled. Her slip showed from beneath her gray skirt. Her makeup was on, but not in place, so that the rouge was too high on her cheekbones, the lipstick a red mustache above her upper lip.

She peered uncertainly at the desk in the corner. It was surrounded by a huddle of men. She didn't see Dina Forrest's red head.

June thought that maybe she'd leave, forget why she'd come here. She was already late for work. Not that Richard Braun would bawl her out. He never did. He was no Red Stanton. Besides, Richard had troubles of his own to think about. He probably wouldn't even notice that she wasn't there yet. He'd hardly talked to her, given her any work these last couple of weeks.

Willie Harker came toward her. At the same time the huddle around the desk broke open. She saw Dina.

"Morning, June," Willie said. "Something I can do for you?"

She walked past him as if she hadn't heard a word he'd said. He didn't realize what she was up to until she planted herself in front of Dina's desk.

"I'm June," she said in a half-whisper. "June Stanton. Red's wife."

Dina looked up at her, a small thin smile on her lips, her eyes sparkling. "I guess you know me."

"No. I don't. And I don't want to. What I came for is . . . I want to tell you to stay away from my husband from now on."

Willie started for June, then stopped. He didn't know what to do, whether to go break it up before they got into a catfight that tore up the office, or just stand there and watch.

"Maybe you should tell your husband to stay away from me," Dina said, laughing.

Willie was shocked. He'd never seen her like that, with that look on her face. She'd always been sweet, flirty, teasing. Good for business. She was teasing still, but something mean showed through. Mean, and tough as nails. It made Willie very uncomfortable.

June stared at Dina for a long, slow moment, her face blank. Then she said slowly, "But it's not right. We've been together a long time." She stopped, as if confused. Then: "A long time," she repeated, unsure of how long actually. "And I love him."

"Maybe you better tell *him*," Dina said. "I don't run your man for you. What makes you think I do? I never chased him.

191

Why should I? It was the other way around. Him chasing me. And, as a matter of fact, I'd just as soon he'd quit bothering me."

"Then why don't you leave him alone?"

"Maybe I will," Dina said softly. "Maybe I'll do just that. If I want to, that is." She was thinking of Claude. It wasn't really a maybe. She didn't need Red Stanton any more. He was a minus rather than a plus. She looked up at June, still smiling. Dina wasn't angry. She wasn't afraid. June didn't matter. And in a way, a way she didn't understand, it was fun to sit here, with everybody watching, and tell off Red Stanton's wife. "Keep him home, if you can. But don't blame me. If I hadn't come along, there'd have been somebody else."

June wanted to answer, to say a lot more. But as she stood there she forgot that. She was suddenly scared. Really scared. Dina Forrest wasn't embarrassed or ashamed. She was saying in effect that if she wanted Red she'd keep him. Since she didn't June could have him. Her smile was saying that June was nobody and nothing and didn't matter. Shuddering, June turned away.

Willie said good-bye to her. "Take it easy," he called after her, but she ran outside without answering. She ran all the way to Richard's office, and spent the day staring out of the window, wondering what was the matter with her and what was going to happen.

Dina wasn't in her room so Red went down to the Hideaway. She was sitting up at the bar, talking to Pete Burger.

He stopped in the doorway. The way she sat on the bar stool, her legs crossed, and one foot swinging . . . The way her red head tipped to one side . . . Jesus! Exactly like Maggie! He

192

almost turned to go. But then he asked himself what the hell was the matter with him? Sometimes people looked like each other. Maybe everybody in the world had a double someplace.

He went to her. "I was looking for you."

"And now you've found me." She smiled, but she didn't seem glad to see him.

"What's the matter?" he asked.

"Nothing."

"How about tonight?"

"No." Just that. Flat out.

"Aw, come on, Dina. What's wrong? We can have a good time." He sounded like a small boy, begging. He knew it and it made him mad.

"Have you seen your wife lately?" she asked.

"What? What about her?"

"Your wife. June. That fat blond you're married to. Have you seen her lately?"

"What's this about?" he demanded. He saw from the corner of his eye that Pete was listening. Red lowered his voice, leaned closer to her.

Tilting away from him, she said, "Go away, Red."

"What's going on?"

"I don't like people's wives to come to my job and to try to make trouble for me," Dina said sharply. "I don't like people's wives being mean. I think a man ought to keep his wife off the necks of other girls. That's what I think. Now do you know what I mean?"

"No. I don't. Make some sense," he growled.

"I've just told you. She came to Willie Harker's today and told me to stay away from you. Which I will do from now on. I don't know you, Red. Not any more. I thank you for finding me in the lot, and taking me to the hospital, and getting me the job. I thank you very much. Only now I don't know you any more. There. Does that make sense?"

Color crawled up his neck. His forehead shone over the green Indian band that held his long hair in place. "To hell with her," he said hoarsely. "She doesn't tell me what to do."

"I don't care," Dina said. "Just leave me alone."

"It's Claude," Red said slowly. "You're blaming June. But it's actually Claude, isn't it?"

"That's right," she agreed sweetly. "And so what?"

Pete decided he'd better break it up. "Anybody for a drink here?" he asked, with a warning look at Red.

Red turned on his heel and walked out. Instead of going directly home, he stopped at the Glass Slipper. A lot of his friends were there, but he sat alone. He drank beer for two hours, pouring it down straight from the can as soon as he was served, and brooding over Dina Forrest. The way, for just a minute, she'd reminded him of Maggie. How it had all seemed like a run-through of something he'd known from before. How she sounded. How she looked. A lot of what she'd said. The feeling that he'd been there before, heard it before. Damn Claude. She couldn't really go for that crackpot. Damn him!

Red was still boiling when he got home. He slammed the door open and kicked it shut after him. He stopped short when he saw the two packed suitcases in the middle of the room. June was sitting at the table, her head in her hands.

"I was just waiting for you to come back," she said.

"Why did you do it?" he demanded.

She knew what he meant and didn't pretend not to. "Be-cause . . . because I didn't want you going around with her.

194

That's why. Because I can't stand it. Either we're together. Or we're not."

"You know, you're crazy. What I do, that's my business."

"Sure. Okay. That's what you've always told me. Only it's my business too. You want her? Right. Take her. But I'm not going to stand still and watch it."

His boil became a simmer. If she'd yelled at him, he'd have yelled back. But she was talking quietly. He jerked out a chair, sat opposite her. "Why couldn't you just let it go?"

"Because no matter what I've said, I love you."

"Oh, shut up, June. That's got nothing to do with it."

She got to her feet. "I might as well leave now."

"Where for?"

"I don't know."

"You don't have to." He meant it. He couldn't imagine her managing to live her life without him around to look after her.

She looked at him.

He wriggled his wrist so that the tattooed snake crawled from under his sleeve. He expected her to giggle at that the way she always did. This time she wasn't paying attention.

Finally he spoke. "I told you, you don't have to leave. You won. It's finished with her. You did just what you wanted to do. She's through with me. I won't be seeing her any more."

June let her breath out slowly. "I'm glad."

"You don't get the credit for it. So don't think you do. It's something else. Dina's found better pickings."

"There's something funny about that girl," June said. She wondered how to put it. Looking into her eyes had scared June, but she didn't know how to put the feeling into words. She went on. "She's trouble, Red. Something's not right."

"You hophead. What do you know?"

"I might have been before, but not any more. And I'm getting better. I know I am. I can feel it. But maybe because of what I used to be I can sense things. There's something not right with her. Like a girl I knew that went bad on LSD. And it kept flashing back on her. Even years later. It's like that with Dina. And it scares me."

He shrugged, got up to carry her suitcases into the tiny bedroom. "Aw, forget it," he said finally. "She's got nothing to do with you, June."

But he was thinking of Claude, cursing him in his mind. He forgot the recreation center. He forgot what good he could do the town if Claude Vickery took off. He was thinking of himself, of Dina Forrest. And wondering what would happen if Claude left Meadowville for good. There was only one way, Red decided, to find out.

It was the day before Thanksgiving. A black cloud hung over Dead Man's Bluff, and it was snowing when the UPS truck skidded up Vickery Street and stopped at Claude's door.

He heard the ring of the bell, put a few lines more on the drawing paper, then went to answer it.

He frowned, accepting the package. It had to be a drawing, a strip. He could see that from its shape. It was exactly like what he always sent to the syndicate in New York. One set every week. Friday at the same time. Only this one had the syndicate's return address on it.

He took the package into his studio and carefully opened it. He couldn't believe his eyes at what he saw. They had sent the last strip back. He didn't know why. There was no note attached. And as far as he could see, there was nothing wrong with the work either. The long distance call came while he was still poring over it.

"Hey, Claude. How you doing out there?"

"Okay," he said. "We're having the first snow of the season."

"Did you vote for Reagan?"

"Mind your own business."

There was the usual banter. Nothing strange about it. But there was something a little unnerving about the silence that followed.

The editor cleared his throat. "You get the work back yet? I stalled talking to you, hoping you'd get to see it first."

"It just came today. What's the matter?"

"Have you looked at it?"

"Sure I looked. What's going on?"

"I thought you'd see it right away. You know I can't pass it on the way it is. You've got a whole new character in there. And no introduction. No work-up. No nothing. There she is, right in the middle of the action. No rhyme to it, no reason. It can't happen like that. The reader won't stand for it."

"Wait," Claude said, and put down the phone. Now when he looked at the strip he saw what he'd missed before. How he could have, he didn't know. Why it had happened, he didn't know either. But right there, as the editor had said, right there in the middle of the strip, was Maggie. A rush of tears stung his eyes and sweat broke out on his face. He dropped the strip to the drawing board, went back to the phone. He had to swallow hard before he could speak. "I'll fix it fast and get it back to you."

"Sure," the editor said. "And when will you be coming home?"

"I don't know. It's going to be a while." He'd never been specific about when he would be returning. He hadn't liked the idea of burning his bridges behind him. Now he was glad. He'd only been in Meadowville six or seven weeks. It already seemed like forever. He didn't let himself think about what two years would feel like. He was going to stay. He was entitled to what was his, and he was going to get it. And anyhow, he couldn't leave any more. Not even if he wanted to. There was Dina.

He put down the phone and went to work on the strip immediately. It meant doing it all over again. He checked it three times before he finished it, then packed it and took it out to mail.

It was the same clerk as usual at the window. "You're off schedule, aren't you?" he said.

Claude didn't answer, passed the money, and went out, thinking that the clerk ought to mind his own business. What if it was Wednesday instead of Friday?

At home, with the snow still falling, he picked up the phone to call Willie Harker's to talk to Dina. There was no dial tone. He jiggled the phone, tried it again. Dead. He heard the snow beating against the big window and thought that maybe a line was down somewhere.

He pulled on a vest, a heavy down jacket, and drove over to Richard's office. From there he reported that his phone was out of order. He stayed a little while, but Richard was preoccupied and didn't seem to want to visit, so Claude went home.

He worked for a few hours. When he got up from the drawing board, stretching his tired shoulders, the window was dark.

He tried the phone again and found that it was all right. He called Dina's room to ask her if she'd go out with him but there was no answer.

He changed clothes, thinking he'd go down to the Hilton anyway. Maybe she was just getting home from work late because of the weather.

But Dina had been there when the phone rang. She hadn't answered it. She hadn't felt like talking to anybody who was calling her. There was only one person she felt like talking to. That was Liz Paige. It was crazy how all day long she'd wanted to call Liz. Only what for? What was she going to say? So she didn't answer the phone.

And now she felt funny, though she didn't know what was wrong. She walked restlessly around the room before going to the mirror. That red hair. She just wasn't sure. It was so short it made her neck feel cold. Sometimes she liked it, and felt it was just right. And sometimes when she looked at herself in the mirror she didn't know who she was. This was one of those times. That red hair gave her the creeps.

She wandered to the closet. All that space wasted on things she never wore, couldn't imagine ever wearing. Maybe she should throw them out. She'd thought of that a lot. But when it came down to doing it, she found she couldn't. A whole wardrobe like that, stuff she'd worn in a time she couldn't remember. She'd been Dina Forrest then too, but who was Dina Forrest? It was so peculiar. So downright not normal. She wished she knew what was the matter with her. And she wished she knew why it mattered.

She sat down at the dressing table, creamed her face, took off all her makeup. Drab. No color. No excitement. Like a schoolteacher. But it felt good. Nice and clean. Maybe that's how she'd been in her other life. Nice. Clean. Liz Paige had said *she'd* want to know, have to know, would have gone back to New York . . .

Dina slowly pulled her suitcase from the closet. She'd do it. It was right. She'd feel better once she'd been back there. Just a quick visit. One day. Two. It was all she'd need.

The suitcase suddenly swung and twisted in her hand, then shot away from her. Her knees collapsed. She fell on the bed. The room spun around her. Her head ached. Tears came to her eyes. She pressed her hands to her temples, seeing the yellow walls of the hospital. The nurse was saying, "Hello, Ms. Forrest." What a funny way to be born.

But she couldn't stand thinking about it for too long. She jumped up, stumbling over the suitcase. What on earth was she thinking about? She didn't want to go back to New York. Not now. Not when everything was going just right. She stuck the bag in the closet where she couldn't see it. She didn't think about Liz Paige or about what she had said.

Dina showered, made up her face, dressed in a silky new slip, combed her red hair and put on a new dress. She was going to have to stop buying clothes. It was silly, she thought, the way she spent every cent as she earned it. She ought to put a little in the bank at least. Start an account. Think about getting a room somewhere. As she'd done before, she promised herself she'd turn over a new leaf. That's what she'd do. Quit buying so many clothes. Start saving. Get a room maybe.

But it wasn't so important. After all, there was Claude. She stretched over the bed, took up the brown bear, hugged it to her. Claude had plenty of money and pretty soon he'd have more. She smiled to herself. He was falling in love with her.

And that was what she wanted. She knew it. What she wanted was Claude.

It didn't surprise her that he called from downstairs as she sat there, hugging the bear. She guessed she'd been expecting him to.

She went down to meet him, saw the eager way he stared at her as she crossed the lobby. They kissed when they were in the car. A good deep kiss. She felt his tongue in her mouth before she drew away, laughing.

"Now, Claude, what are we going to do?"

He wanted to go for a ride but the Volare wouldn't start. He tinkered with it, swearing, stamping around in the snow until his boots were soaked through and his trousers were wet to the knees. It didn't help. She was ready to give it up, go in and have a drink at the Hide-away. But Claude said no way. He'd get it going no matter what.

Half an hour later Red's pickup pulled into the parking lot and stopped. Red climbed out, grinning. He watched Claude bend over the engine.

"Trouble, Claude?"

"It won't start," Claude said through gritted teeth.

"Let me look." Red bent over. "Yeah, sure. Look here. You've got a loose wire."

Claude brushed snowflakes from his glasses, peered in. "It's been cut," Red said, laughing. "Look here where it's shiny. You got any enemies, Claude?"

Claude didn't answer. He twisted the cut wires together, slammed down the hood.

Red opened the car door, looked in at Dina. "You haven't wasted any time. But that's okay. Whatever you want is okay with me. Only remember I told you first. You be careful of this guy."

"Mind your own business," she said archly.

He laughed and walked away, saying over his shoulder to Claude, "And you be careful too. Don't go riding again on Dead Man's Bluff."

Claude fell into the car. His face was wet. Snow, he told himself. But it was hot, salty. It was sweat mixed with tears. He was churning inside. Damn Red. What was he trying to do?

Dina put her hand on his knee, snuggled close. "Hey, Claude, hey sweetie, pay some attention to me."

With a groan, he folded her into his arms. Her scent was sweet, familiar. Her body was soft, warm, familiar too. He was holding Maggie in his arms again. The way he'd wished for ten years of his life. He was holding Maggie, and she was his.

A shrill screaming siren. A rising wail, a falling moan.

Claude rolled his head on the pillow. The dream, the dream . . .

The squeal of wheels, voices, a pounding at the door.

He jerked upright. He was awake. The noise was real.

As he grabbed a robe, he saw swinging red and white dome lights. They flashed through the dark room, faded, flashed again. Men's shouts echoed.

He grabbed a robe, rushed downstairs and threw open the door.

A lifted fist, poised to the bang the panel again, dropped. "Where is it?" a man yelled.

"Where's what?" he asked, bewildered. The red and white lights continued to skim by. Metallic sounds hung on the still air. "What?" he repeated.

"The injured party." The two men on the threshold stared at him. The speaker said more quietly, "We had a call." He jerked a thumb over his shoulder at the rescue squad truck in the driveway behind him.

Claude shook his head, stammered that he'd made no call.

"A shooting," the man said. "Vickery Street."

"No," Claude whispered, choking. "No. There's nothing like that here."

"Somebody playing games," the man muttered.

But the other one pushed a button on a small black box. "Hey, control. Give me a reading on that last emergency call."

"Vickery Street," the box said. "A shooting."

The men looked at each other, shrugged.

"Sorry to roll you out at this hour."

Claude nodded, closed the door.

A shooting. A false report. The rescue squad screaming through the night.

He dragged himself back to his bedroom, slid under the blanket, shivering.

A false call. On Halloween, garbage had been thrown in his yard, six cans of it scattered in contempt. Tonight the wire in his Volari had been cut, so it wouldn't start. And now, the sirens blasting through the night.

He knew. But he wouldn't let himself think about it. He pulled the pillows over his head so he wouldn't see the red and white lights swing through the room as the truck moved slowly up and down the street. Looking. Just to be sure. Looking. Just in case.

He was still scared when he woke up the next morning. Someone had deliberately called the false alarm in, sent the rescue squad to his house. Someone had said there'd been a shooting. That meant whoever it was had been thinking about guns, thinking about a shooting.

He was still scared, but nothing happened.

He told himself they weren't going to run him off. He had come back because of Maggie. And now he had her.

But, of course, he actually meant Dina.

The Sunday papers came in late because of the weather. But by afternoon, the sun was out and the roads were finally clear again.

Claude stood on his porch in his shirt-sleeves, looking at his strip, "Vick." He looked at it, then blinked and looked away. Blinking again, he checked it one last time. No use. It was just as he'd thought the first time. A crazy thing had happened.

They'd run the wrong one. There, right in the middle of the strip, without rhyme or reason, was Maggie's face.

He went inside, slammed the door. He paced the room for hours. How in the hell! What kind of a mistake was that? He'd gotten the strip back, corrected it, returned it. And Maggie was still there. It was done. It couldn't be taken back. Everybody in town was going to see it. Everybody would recognize Maggie Paige's face.

Soon the whole town knew about it. Richard saw it and shook his head, wondering uneasily how it had happened and what Claude was thinking of. Liz saw it a little later and burst into tears. Red saw it and laughed and showed it to June. When Dina saw it she thought Claude had drawn her.

Willie Harker told Vernon Meese that it was Claude's way of telling the town to go to hell. Vernon told his wife that Claude ought to be wrapped in a white jacket and sent back to where he'd been before.

204

Nobody mentioned it to Claude. But he didn't have to be told. He knew what they were all thinking.

He knew what his editor was beginning to think, too. He had called to raise hell because the mistake had been made. The corrected strip had been lost and the old one used. That's how he finally explained it to himself. The editor patiently explained that the strip used was the new one. That's how it had come in, so that's how they'd gone with it, thinking it was what Claude wanted after all. Claude apologized and promised to have something new in the mail within a few days.

He worked hard, stopping only for a few hours each night to have dinner with Dina, to go riding with her, to walk along Main Street, to go dancing, his head bent to hers at the country club.

He knew that everybody in town was watching them, talking about them. He didn't care. It was all so familiar. The way it had been ten years before.

He remembered it clearly. How he'd felt about her. How she'd felt about him. A Vickery and a Paige. And nothing else mattered. That he stammered was nothing. That he was skinny and graceless and a bookworm didn't matter. She loved him. Maggie loved him. He'd correct himself then. Dina loved him. But gradually over the days, he forgot to correct himself. Maggie loved him. Maggie, come back from the grave.

The next Sunday he was almost afraid to look at the strip. But it was okay. He was relieved that he'd gotten himself straightened out. He spent the evening with Richard, bowling. He didn't mention the false shooting report. And Richard didn't ask him how things were going.

He knew Richard had plenty of things on his mind. His practice was shrinking. Liz and he still didn't seem to be talking

205

about getting married, although Claude knew that was what Richard wanted more than anything else. On Monday morning the work Claude had mailed earlier was returned. Every character in the strip was Maggie.

He put it under a magnifying glass to look at it through blurring tears. It was his work all right. Nobody else but his. His hand. His line.

He'd drawn Maggie. Six characters, and all of them nobody but Maggie.

After a while, gritting his teeth, he went to work again.

Chapter 16

That Sunday Claude picked Dina up at the Hilton, then drove to a place called Gaynor's for champagne brunch. She wore her black velveteen coat and high-heeled red suede boots. Her hair blazed around her face over her shining eyes.

She was clinging to his arm, and as they passed a tall Christmas tree standing in the corner she pulled him to a stop, reaching out to touch a glowing yellow ribbon.

"That's nice," she said. "For the hostages." And: "I always loved Christmas." A sudden shiver went over her as she spoke the words. Had she? How did she know? She didn't remember any Christmas before. This would be the first one. Then she giggled. It really was like being newly born.

"We'll do something special to celebrate," he told her.

As the hostess led them to a table in the middle of the room, they passed Vernon Meese and his wife. Claude nodded, Dina smiled widely, but Vernon didn't speak.

When they were seated, Dina said thoughtfully, "You don't

have many friends in this town, do you? Not for having lived here all your life."

He looked at her across the table, aware of Vernon's eyes watching him, knowing that everybody in the place was staring at him. He wished they'd been given a corner table. He wished he hadn't brought her to Gaynor's.

She grinned. "Oh, don't look like that. I don't care if you have friends."

So he told her about the accident in which Maggie Paige had died. He told her about the institution, and coming out cured, and going on to New York to make a new life for himself. And he told her about John's will. All the time he was talking there was, somewhere in his mind, a voice saying it wasn't necessary to go on about it. Maggie already knew. Surely Maggie already knew.

Dina sat very still, her ankles crossed beneath the table, her hands cupping her chin. She didn't hear anything he said. But that didn't matter. She'd already heard it all before. They'd told her at Willie Harker's. Willie and his salesmen. Even Pete Burger at the Hilton Hide-away. They'd all told her about Claude Vickery. How there'd been an accident on Dead Man's Bluff and how beautiful redheaded Maggie Paige had died. How Claude had been locked up for three years. And nobody had heard from him for the ten years he'd been gone. And about how he came back because his brother left him a lot of money if he'd stay in Meadowville for two years, and gave it to the town if he didn't. They told her also about the peculiar coincidence. He'd gone to visit Liz's mother, and spent a couple of hours talking with her, and that very night Mrs. Paige had died. They'd even told her how Maggie's face had turned up in the strip he drew, although she'd known about that, seen

208

it for herself. Telling her, they were warning her, just as Red had warned her. Against Claude. And that was funny, though she didn't know why. That they should warn *her* against *him*. So she knew all about it. Not that it mattered to her.

But she didn't hear his halting explanation because something seemed to happen to her ears. There was a buzzing and rumbling in them. His voice seemed far away and full of static. And she could hardly see his face, either. Because a mist had fallen between them. She was looking through what seemed a curtain of snow.

It was like being there and not being there. A terrible sensation. She wanted to laugh. She wanted to scream. She thought, for a minute or two, that her mind would go blank, her head split wide open and allow her brains to spill out onto the white tablecloth. Yet she sat still, with her hands folded under her chin.

Vernon watched, narrow eyed, from across the room. He saw Claude's lips moving, Dina's intent face.

"I'll bet they're sleeping together," Vernon's wife said.

"It doesn't matter."

"We don't like such goings-on in this town. Maybe it's all right in New York. But it isn't all right here."

Vernon wasn't listening. He watched Claude and thought that Claude was a lot stronger than Vernon had given him credit for. He knew everything that had happened. The garbage in the front yard, the Volare's occasional breakdowns, the false call to the rescue squad reporting a shooting. Everybody in town knew. Just as everybody had seen Maggie's face peering out of the comics and believed that meant Claude was beginning to crack up. But he was still in Meadowville. It was, Vernon thought, time to give his oranges a little more push.

He decided he'd get together with Red the next morning. Not that Vernon was going to say anything directly. He'd never risk himself that way. But he would find a way to get Red moving. Red, or maybe one of his friends. He finished his coffee and pushed back his chair, smiling. He liked the idea of being a juggler.

In the middle of the room, Claude seemed to run down, his lips no longer moving. He looked anxiously at Dina. Waiting. What would she say? His Maggie. What would she say now that she knew how it had been since she died? He wasn't aware that more and more often he thought of Dina as Maggie. Thought of her as *his* Maggie, who had come back to him. And forgot that she was Dina Forrest whom he'd met at the bar in the Hilton Hide-away.

She remained silent, her eyes fixed on his.

Finally he said, "Now you know all about it."

She heard that. The buzzing was gone from her ears. Her vision was clearing. She saw the look on his face at last, and understood it instantly.

She laughed, and everybody in the room looked at her. Aware of their stares she leaned forward and took Claude's hand. "I've known from the beginning," she said, and with a jerk of her bright head she added, "They made sure, believe me."

He sagged in his chair. "I figured, but hoped not."

"You know what?" She tightened her fingers. "You know what, Claude? They're all crazy. That's what I think."

A grin split his lips. His feet shuffled under the table in a quick dance. "You're wonderful, Dina."

Yet what he was thinking—as he thought it so many times through the years—was *You're wonderful, Maggie.* Because, of

210

course, she was. She was wonderful. And she was Maggie. That sweet familiarity that had charmed him at first was stronger than ever now.

Maybe it wasn't the right place. And it was rather early on as well. But he didn't care. He had to say it. He took a deep breath.

"Listen, Dina, you know how much I love you. Let's get married."

Her eyes met his full on. A faint smile moved across her lips.

The silence stretched out between them. He thought it spread from moments to hours. He could hear his heart beat and feel his pores sweat and it was as if he'd waited just the same way before, held his breath, hoping to hear her say, "Yes."

She said slowly, "We haven't known each other very long."

"I knew the first time I saw you," he answered. "I always knew." And to himself he thought: *Oh, Maggie, how can it be sudden? Don't you remember the way it was?*

"Yes," she said.

He stared at her, uncertain of what she meant. "Yes," but to what?

"Yes," she repeated, laughing. "I'll marry you." She was delighted. It was exactly what she intended. But still . . . she didn't know what to call it . . . she had a funny shaky feeling inside.

He jumped to his feet and whooped as loud as he could. He hollered, loping around the table to her. He grabbed her out of her chair and swung her into his arms. Half-laughing, half-crying, he told her that he loved her, had always loved her. And over his shoulder, she stuck out her tongue at the audience that watched with avid eyes.

211

Then, when he had put her on her feet, he grabbed two glasses of champagne from the tray of a passing waitress and toasted her, and the audience, shouting, "Dina and I are going to get married. Isn't that wonderful!"

. . . Later, when Liz told him about it, Richard burst out laughing.

Liz hadn't thought it was funny when Mrs. Baldwin described the scene as she had heard about it from Vernon Meese's wife. She didn't think so now.

"That was an extraordinary performance," Liz said. "And how can he and Dina be getting married? They hardly know each other."

Richard sobered quickly. "Maybe that's what it takes. Not knowing each other too long." He waited for her to say something. When she didn't, he went on. "I've known you for what, twelve years or so, isn't it? And we've been talking about marriage for two years. And now, now that we can, you're stalling."

"I've explained that. You ought to understand." Her body ached. Her eyes stung. She wished she hadn't mentioned Claude and Dina at all.

"But I don't understand. Maybe you'd better explain it to me again."

"I just need a little more time." She was whispering without knowing that she was. If only she dared tell him . . . but she had tried, and he had brushed away her words. Just as she had once brushed away her mother's words. But they had kept coming back, and Liz couldn't ignore them any more. Her mother had been certain when Claude returned to Meadowville that Maggie would return, too. And there was Dina . . . Dina, with the flaming red hair and dancing walk, to whom

212

Liz was drawn, by whom Liz was repelled. Dina, who had a brown bear like the one Maggie had always cuddled in her arms before going to sleep.

"Don't wait too long," Richard was saying.

She didn't answer. She sensed the growing width of the chasm between them, and it frightened her. If she couldn't talk to the man she loved, then who could she talk to?

"I'll phone Claude tomorrow to congratulate him," Richard said, smiling wryly.

"If only he hadn't stayed," she answered. "If only he hadn't come from New York when you called him."

Red was shaken when he heard about it. His scarred face turned crimson. But what swept him wasn't jealousy. Once the break with Dina had come, he'd found that he was relieved. It was as if a heavy and dangerous weight had leaned on him. Now it was gone. There was something pretty kooky about Dina, he thought, when you got right down to it. She gave him the willies. Just like Claude. The two of them deserved each other.

It was, instead, the recreation center that Red was thinking of now. He didn't see why the town had to be beat out of what it was due by Claude Vickery. He made sure that everyone he talked to knew what was on his mind. But he didn't tell anybody what he was planning to do.

Chapter 17

By mid-December both the third heavy snowstorm of the season and Iran's conditions for release of the hostages were taking second place to talk about Claude.

The comic strips in which Maggie had appeared were hashed over. The coincidence of Ellen Paige's death just after his return was remarked. The accident in which Maggie had died was brought up all over again. His looks, the wild light in his eyes, his lurching walk. His coming marriage to a girl who didn't even know who she was. His decision to stay and inherit John Vickery's property when everybody knew Claude wasn't entitled to it. The consensus was that he was crazy and ought to be locked up, or at least run out of town on a rail.

Mostly it was talk. But not all of it.

Vernon Meese and Willie Harker had a quiet conversation.

"We've got to remember," Vernon said, "It's a question of the town or him."

"And he's a nut," Willie answered, knuckling his jaw. "He always was, even when he was a kid. Now he's worse."

"He ought to be back in the funny farm."

Willie nodded assent. "But saying isn't doing."

They went first to Dr. Detrick. He listened, then shook his head. "I don't know what you're talking about. And neither do you. There's nothing actionable in Claude Vickery's behavior."

"You don't understand," Vernon Meese said. "He's a menace to the town."

"That's right," Willie said. "If you'd seen him swing that girl around in Gaynor's. And the way she stuck out her tongue at everybody."

"If you put people away for that, then you'd have to both be locked up." Dr. Detrick smiled. "I remember you, Willie, when you were a boy."

"He's no boy." Vernon smoothed back his blond hair. "Claude's a grown man."

"If he was a danger to himself, to anyone else, it would be different." Dr. Detrick stood up. "But he's not. At least nothing you've told me makes me think he is. And now, if you don't mind . . ."

Outside the office, Vernon said, "Old fool! It's time he retired."

Willie scuffed his boots in the snow. "What now?"

"We're going to talk to Richard."

"And he's going to say . . ."

"I know what he's going to say. But maybe he'll pass the message on to Claude."

When Richard heard the two men out he was first inclined to laugh. But then he grew sober. They really meant it. Claude was crazy. He was a menace to the town. Look at all the things he did. He ought to be put away for his own safety. And there was a way. He would be declared incompetent on Richard's say-

215

so. And Richard could have his power of attorney. The town wouldn't forget what Richard had done for it.

Richard answered them coldly. "I've known you men all my life, and I realize now that I never knew you at all."

"It's for his own good," Willie said defensively. "You stop and think about it. You never know what he's going to do next. And there was Maggie . . ."

"That was an accident," Richard protested. "And he was a kid."

"And Mrs. Paige. No finer woman ever walked the face of the earth."

"She was a very sick person, and had been for years. He had nothing to do with her death."

"Only broke her heart," Vernon said flatly. "At the least. And he was there, wasn't he?"

Richard stood up. "Forget it. And remember, if you try an end run, you're going to have to go past me. I'm not going to let you pull any funny legal maneuvers on Claude."

He had hardly finished when the door burst open.

Claude stood there, panting. He was coatless, tieless. His hair stood straight up and his face was pale. His eyes burned behind his glasses. He tried to speak, but couldn't. The words were stuck in his throat.

"What's the matter?" Richard asked quickly. "What happened?"

Claude divided a desperate look between Willie and Vernon.

They rose promptly, told Richard they had to go, but lingered in the door, curiosity holding them against the push of embarrassment.

"What's the matter?" Richard asked again.

"My window," Claude finally brought it out. He still didn't believe what had happened. He was still too shocked to be angry. That would come later. Now, bewildered and frightened, he wanted to tell Richard about it, but not with Vernon Meese and Willie Harker there.

Richard understood. He turned to the men. "See you again soon." Saying that, he brushed shoulders with them, moving them outside. To June he said, "Show Mr. Meese and Mr. Harker out, will you?"

"We know the way," Willie said.

But June smiled and opened the door, and when the two men had gone, she closed it firmly and loudly.

As soon as Richard had seated himself, Claude clenched his unsteady hands on his knees. "I was sitting there working. It was going good for a change. And thinking of Dina." It had been Maggie he'd been thinking about, but he didn't say that. "And the window exploded. It blew up over my head. Shards of glass flying like shrapnel. It's a wonder I wasn't killed."

"Change of temperature?" Richard asked.

Claude thrust his hand into his shirt pocket. He dropped two spent shells on the desk. Richard whistled softly.

"I heard a car drive away," Claude told him.

"Get the license plate?"

"No." It had happened so fast. One minute he was concentrating on the drawing paper before him. The next . . . flying glass . . . a hum of tires . . . When he looked into the street, it was empty.

"We'll get to the bottom of it." Richard reached for the phone. "The police . . ."

217

"Police!" Claude was up on his feet, pacing now. Two tiger steps one way. Two tiger steps another. A fist pounding his hip. "Wait, Richard. No police."

"You have to."

Claude shook his head. No, not the police. He was almost crying. He felt sobs building up in his chest. Not the police. He remembered too well. The hard stares. The questions, always the same, over and over again. What happened? What were you doing? Why were you driving on Dead Man's Bluff? How fast were you going? As if it was his fault. His. And Maggie was lying there. Dead. His Maggie. "No police, Richard," he said finally, voice and body shaking.

"You have to," Richard repeated. He remembered thinking once that the town resented Claude's coming back to claim his inheritance, but that there was nothing it could do. The town was showing him now how wrong he'd been. There was plenty it could do.

"No police," Claude was saying. He went to the door. It had been a mistake to come here. He'd had to tell someone, he supposed. That's why he'd come. Just to say it. But he oughtn't to have done it. He'd always been a loner. He still was. Now the anger came, hot and fast, like water suddenly boiling into steam. It was the town. Sweet on the outside. Rotten on the inside. It was trying to cheat him, drive him away. The garbage, the false rescue squad report of a shooting. And now the real shooting. Only the town didn't know he was different now. He was stronger. He could handle it. He wasn't going to let it ruin him.

"All right," Richard said. "If you insist. I'll see what I can do. Ask around. Maybe we can handle it that way." He thought it possible. He had contacts in the police, in the courthouse.

Someone might know what was going on. Obviously the feelings in the town were stirred up. And there were Vernon and Willie Harker to begin with.

But his questions didn't do any good. Vernon and Willie stared at him indignantly. They'd been together having coffee when it happened. Or else they'd been with Richard in his office. They were respectable businessmen, and who the hell was he to accuse them? He wasn't, he assured them. He'd just thought they might have heard a small something. Both men thought of Red Stanton, and didn't mention his name.

They didn't need to. Richard had already thought of him. Red was more than willing to talk to Richard. He said where he'd been all that day. Things were tough in the construction trade. He didn't have work. He couldn't sit home and stare at four walls so he'd gone out to the Glass Slipper. He told Richard to go and ask. But he wanted Richard to know that whatever happened to Claude was okay with him. Only he hadn't done anything, and Richard couldn't prove he had.

Richard never knew how close he was to the truth behind the unspoken conspiracy. Vernon and Willie had done nothing but talk. They'd told Red that if Claude married Dina, the town could kiss its inheritance good-bye. Together they'd stick it out to get what wasn't rightfully theirs. So forget the recreation center. Red didn't do anything but talk either. He told an assembled group of unemployed construction workers about how Claude had all that New York money coming to him every month and how, in a couple of years, he'd have all the Vickery property and the town would be out of its center as well as a good clean industry that would have brought in maybe twelve hundred jobs.

While he was talking about it, pounding a callused fist on

the bar, two men slipped away.

They got into a nondescript pickup, took guns from the overhead rack and drove out to Claude's. About three-quarters of an hour later they returned, smiling, and ordered up a bottle of Heavenly Hill. It turned out to be a pretty good party.

But Richard never heard anything about that. When he left Red, he knew no more than he had before. He checked out his other resources. They didn't help, either. What he had to go on were suspicions, and nothing else.

When nothing happened over the next day or two, he began to hope that it had been a freak outburst, and that was the end of it.

He didn't realize that plenty was happening.

CHAPTER 18

Claude had made up his mind not to tell anybody what was going on. Not Dina—it might scare her and make her change her mind about marrying him. Not Richard because he might go to the police no matter how Claude protested. And those two were all he had. So it was easy to keep quiet. In the beginning at least.

The day after the big window had been shot out in front of him eighty-five dollars worth of fresh flowers were delivered with a sympathy card saying, "We regret your loss." He threw them away. Two hours later he found that all four tires on the Volare had been slashed. He bought replacements at Willie Harker's. Shortly after he got home fourteen cases of beer were delivered. He paid for them without complaint. He also paid for twenty-two steaks that arrived a little later. When he added it up, he decided he'd quit that, and did. He sent back the rest of what came. Fruit, by the bushel. Books, by the dozen.

Then the deliveries stopped, and the phone started ringing.

But whenever he picked it up, no one answered. He stopped picking it up.

He told himself not to panic. The thing was to be cool. To ignore it. If they got his goat and knew it, it would keep on going. If they didn't, they'd give up eventually. All he had to do was hang on.

At twilight, when it was snowing again, he got a call from New York. His editor asked about that week's delivery. Claude said it had gone out as usual. The editor told him to check at the post office. It hadn't arrived. It was no problem, he said. They were ahead of schedule. But he told Claude to find out anyway.

Claude got there two minutes before closing time. Red was leaning against the counter, talking to the clerk. He grinned at Claude. "I'm just making sure that Bubba here treats you right."

Claude nodded jerkily. It seemed to him that Red was always there. He'd encountered him just about every week in the past month. But there was nothing he could do about Red hanging around the post office.

Claude asked about the package he'd sent out, showed his receipt. The rabbity-faced clerk looked blank. He didn't know anything about it. He'd put a tracer on it. He shoved forms at Claude, and turned to talk to Red.

When he'd filled out the forms, Claude left, with the laughter of both men trailing him. He felt that every eye in town was tracking him as he drove down Main Street.

The phone rang as soon as he sat down at the drawing board under the boarded-up window. Nobody was there when he answered.

He tried to work, but couldn't. His mind kept going blank.

His hands began to shake. He gave up and went to see Dina.

Then it was all right. When he smiled into her eyes, he knew he was safe. Dina. Maggie. He had her back again.

He drove her to the house, and they watched television together. He wondered if the hostages would ever get back alive. Dina didn't pay any attention. She ate popcorn and licked the melted butter from her fingertips. She knew nothing about current events, and cared even less.

She examined the house with interest, going from room to room almost as if she knew the way. He reminded himself that she didn't. She'd never been there before. But Maggie had. His Maggie had come there often with her parents. It gave him a good feeling to remember. Maggie. Dina. He was sure by now. But he'd never admit it. They'd all think he was crazy. People don't come back from the dead. Though Mrs. Paige had known different. Just as he did. Still, he didn't have to shout it from the rooftops. What was truth was true. And he knew. That was what mattered. He knew he had his Maggie back.

They talked about how they could fix the house up. It needed new furniture, Dina said positively. Something bright, cheerful. The place looked like a morgue. It would be beautiful when she finished with it. She wanted white curtains and velvet drapes and a new white rug. A white rug would be perfect. He said they'd do it up right. Strip off the old wallpaper and paint the walls. They'd get a modern kitchen and a new bathroom. And maybe a swimming pool out back. In the middle of the planning, he stopped.

"Wait, Dina. We haven't set a date."

"December 21," she said promptly, and burst out laughing at the joyful look on his face. "Did you think I was going to change my mind?"

He stood there, feeling the happiness slowly drain out of him. There was suddenly a great vacuum in his head, a vacuum filled with rushing wind. He was dizzy. The room seemed to tilt and sway around him. His legs had become water instead of muscle and bone. He sank into a chair. When she cried, "Claude, what's the matter?" he didn't answer. He didn't know.

She threw herself on his lap and hugged him hard. "Come on, Claude. Let's make more plans. It's so much fun."

While they were talking it hit him that they only had three days in which to get ready. It didn't matter though. There wasn't that much to do, and Richard would help.

Claude told Dina that. She snuggled against him. "Will he be your best man?" Claude nodded. "I wish Liz would be maid of honor," she said.

Claude swallowed. He knew how Liz felt. She'd made it plain.

"That's what I'd really like," Dina said.

He promised he'd ask.

The next day he drove to St. Louis and bought her a diamond wedding ring. And as soon as he returned that evening, he told Richard what he and Dina were planning to do.

He didn't tell Richard about the stream of false deliveries he'd had the day before, the harassing calls that stopped when Dina was with him, then started when he'd returned from taking her home. He didn't tell Richard about the sirens exploding in the street before the house, awakening him from a sound sleep, a sleep of escape from the phone. And how he had leaped from his bed screaming, "Maggie!" And raced downstairs to be confronted by firemen with raised axes shouting, "Where is it?"

He didn't tell Richard because it no longer seemed real to him.

Richard faked an enthusiasm he didn't feel. He wasn't sure in his own mind that it was a good idea. There was too much going on in the town. Claude didn't look well, either. His face was gray and his brown eyes were sunk deep in his head. And Dina had never recovered her memory. Maybe it would be better to wait and see what happened. After all, Richard thought, the attorney in him taking over, she might even already be married. But he didn't want to be a spoiler. He kept his doubts to himself.

And then Claude asked if Richard would be his best man.

Richard grinned. "Sure."

"And . . ." Claude hesitated. He swallowed hard and waited. Even so, it was difficult to get the words out. "Dina wondered . . . that is, she wanted to know . . . would Liz be maid of honor?"

Richard's grin faded. That was something else. He didn't know what to say.

Claude said carefully, "Dina really . . . somehow, I guess, she feels close to Liz." He was thinking of Maggie. Naturally she'd want Liz to be her maid of honor.

"Well, I don't know," Richard said finally. "But I'll ask Liz. Okay?"

Claude looked relieved. "I'd appreciate it. And so would Dina. Oh, I forgot to tell you. It's the day after tomorrow. December 21."

Richard only nodded. December 21. It would be three months to the day since Claude returned to Meadowville for John Vickery's funeral.

Richard spent a major part of the day working out the

arrangements. They were still on his mind when he went to Liz's that evening.

She was tense and very tired. She had been in all day forcing herself to a chore she had delayed too long. She'd packed her mother's clothes for delivery to a senior citizens' home. As she had folded the scarves and sweaters and blouses into cartons, she'd heard her mother's voice again. Sure. Certain. *Maggie will come home.* Liz told herself that she knew it couldn't have happened. Everyone knew that. But . . . but suppose . . . What if she were wrong—if *everybody* were wrong? Suppose something could happen that hardly anyone understood? If Maggie had been able to come back . . . In quick succession, Liz had seen images flash before her. They were of Dina, laughing . . . Dina leaning close to her to peer into her eyes . . . Dina sliding a sidelong glance at Richard . . .

Liz had finally finished the packing and loaded the car. After that she shoveled the walk, hoping the cold air would clear her head.

Richard saw that it had been a bad day for her. He suggested a couple of drinks before dinner. When she left the room to get them, the light seemed to go with her. It was the same for him as when he had first fallen in love with her. But it wasn't the same for her any more.

Since he had promised Claude, Richard told himself that he had to ask Liz. He waited until they'd had a drink. Then when they had started on the second, he told her about Claude's visit and what Claude had said, and hurried on to relay Dina's request.

Liz paled. She spilled half her drink putting it aside. Shifting away from Richard, she ended up huddled in the corner of the sofa, her knees drawn up protectively, her arms folded across

226

her breasts. "I can't," she said. "You should know that. You shouldn't even ask me."

He gave her a quizzical look. "Can't?"

"Can't."

"Don't you mean 'won't'?"

"Can't."

"All right. I asked because I'd promised I would."

"You shouldn't be there, either."

"They're alone," he said. "They've got to have somebody. They're entitled to somebody. They don't have the plague. They're not criminals. They've harmed no one. Why do they have to be treated like lepers? What's wrong with this town?"

But he knew what it was. Greed. And malice. Though he didn't know half of what had happened to Claude, what he did know was enough to disgust him. Meadowville. The town he thought he belonged to. The town he loved. He'd never expected to feel such disgust for his home. He felt it now. Partly for Claude's sake. Partly for his own. Richard was feeling the town's opposition in his bank account. He'd lost ground and stood to lose more.

"You know what's going on," Liz said.

"It doesn't have to affect you too."

She twisted her fingers together so tightly that the tips became noticeably white. Her face had become white too. Her voice was a husky whisper. "I can't have anything to do with Claude. Or with Dina."

"But why? You're not making sense."

"I don't know. I can't. That's all I can tell you." And then, whispering still, "Maybe it's because I'm afraid to, Richard."

He slid close, tried to take her into his arms, but she stiffened, so he knew it was no good. He let his arms fall, but stayed close. "Come on. Tell me. What's scaring you?"

She couldn't look at Richard. How could she explain that she couldn't stand by while Dina took her vows, and cringe inside when Dina smiled, and shrink when Dina laughed? How could she stand there, crazily wondering if Dina Forrest was Maggie. If Maggie had somehow come back to life?

"Liz?" Richard was saying. "Liz?" He put a hand under her chin, tipped her face up and looked into her eyes. He saw terror and shame, and somehow he understood.

He said softly, "Jesus. You're thinking about Maggie, aren't you? Because of Dina. Because she's got red hair. Do you know what that sounds like?"

Liz's mouth tightened. She didn't answer.

"Come on," he said. "Your head is screwed on right. You know how your mother was. You can't let it affect you. And me. Yes, me, Liz."

After a moment, she said coolly, "I don't know what you're talking about. Mom has nothing to do with it."

"Scared. That's what you said, Liz. Of what? Of the ghost of Maggie? Or is it of yourself?"

She ignored that. She said quickly, "You know, I've been thinking of leaving Meadowville. Of maybe going to St. Louis, getting a job. Maybe it's time I tried my wings a little." But just then, while he looked at her, was really the first time she had thought of it. And she knew it was right. With the idea came a lightening of the load she carried. If she went away, she wouldn't be afraid.

"And what about me?" he asked.

"I don't know." But she did know. He'd be better off without her. She remembered her father's drawn face, how tired he had sounded, saying, *Ellen, such things can't be. Maggie won't come back.* She remembered how hard it had been for him to deal with her mother's obsession. It would be just as hard for Richard to deal with hers.

"Liz, what's going on? What are you trying to tell me?"

"It's just that I want to do more than stay in the same old rut."

"You're running away. From me."

"No. Not from you. Just trying to get my bearings, I guess."

"You're running away from me," he repeated. "Just like everybody else in this town, it seems." His grin was bitter. "I thought I belonged here. But maybe it's like with Claude. I don't."

"Is it that bad?"

"Yes." But he didn't tell her how bad. She'd find out soon enough.

"If you dropped Claude . . ."

"I won't do it," Richard said harshly.

"But it would make all the difference. It's only because of him that the town's turned against you."

"And that goes for you too, Liz."

"I'm not against you," she cried.

"But you won't stand with me, either."

"With you and Claude and Dina. That's what you mean."

"It would be for me."

She closed her eyes against stinging tears. He could say whatever he wanted to. There was the red hair, there was the dancing walk and the brown bear and finally there was how she felt within herself. A certain familiarity . . . a longing and a repulsion . . . She said finally, "You don't understand. It's not that I don't want to. It's that I can't."

A little later he left her, and she wondered if she would ever
see him again.

It was the same night. June said, serving the hamburgers and
creamed corn, "I've got to start looking for another job. If you
hear anything, Red, you tell me."

He put down the can of beer he'd been holding. "What are
you talking about now?"

"Richard Braun. He's letting me go. He told me this afternoon."

"What did you do, stupid?"

Her response was automatic. "I don't like for you to call me
that, Red," she said. "I didn't do anything. But nothing's
coming in to pay me."

He wriggled the snake on his wrist, so the blue tattoo seemed
to writhe. She didn't pay any attention to it. "I'll bet you blew
it someway."

"I knew you'd say that. Only it's not me. If anybody blew
it, it was you."

"Me?"

"Talking around town against Claude Vickery until everybody got hot," she said softly. "You think I don't know? Talking against Claude. Putting everybody against Richard. The
bank. The aldermen. Even Willie Harker. All because you
never liked Claude."

Red looked disgusted. "A lot you know."

"I know I'll be out of a job in a couple of weeks. And I liked
it there. I could do it. And Richard Braun was good to me."
Red grunted. "Well, it's true. He has been."

"And I guess I haven't been," Red snapped.

230

"I wasn't talking about you." And then, because Red looked so angry, she went on. "And I guess he knows it's going to get worse. Because Claude and Dina are going to get married day after tomorrow."

Red dropped his beer can. He paid no attention as it rolled across the floor, leaving a trail of foam on the thin rug. "Day after tomorrow? That's crazy!"

"You knew she was going to marry him, so what are you all hot about? She's only set the date. I know because I helped Richard make the arrangements. They're going to the county seat and Judge Rappaport is going to marry them."

"Crazy," Red repeated. He pushed away his uneaten hamburger, got up and walked out.

He drove down to the Hilton and went to Dina's room.

As soon as she opened the door to his knock, he said, "You don't know what you're doing."

"Go away," she told him.

"You're going to be sorry. And I'm not talking because I'm jealous. That's not it. I'm trying to do for you what I owe you. Remember, you told me yourself. About the Chinese. When a man saves your life, then he's responsible for it forever. I'm trying to help you, Dina. You're going to be sorry."

"Sorry for what?" she asked.

"If you marry Claude."

She was holding the brown bear in her arms. She squeezed it tight. "You're a fool, Red Stanton."

"I'm trying to help."

She gave him a wide, warm smile. "Not me, you're not," she said and closed the door in his face as she threw the bear across the room.

He drove home and found June waiting for him. She looked

231

surprised when he came in. He didn't say anything to her. He got a fresh beer from the refrigerator and sat in the big broken chair in front of the television set. He didn't turn it on, but just looked at the blank screen and tried to figure it out. Why he felt so relieved. As if he'd had a narrow escape and just couldn't figure out what he'd gotten away from. It was like a bad dream. You have it . . . You wake up. But you only remember a part of it.

What was in his mind now was that he'd been through this before. Only he didn't remember what it was . . .

"Are you okay?" June asked. She was watching him, her blue eyes wide. Her plump hands were folded in front of her belly, and her plump little feet were toe in. Her slip hung an inch below her skirt on one side. She looked like a kid, a tired and worried kid, who'd been dragged around a shopping center for hours. And that's what she was to him—a kid.

"Red?" she was saying. "Are you okay?"

"Sure." He opened his arms. "Come sit."

She let herself down to his lap and he held her. She was a good weight, and warm. It felt good. He said slowly, "Listen, don't worry about the job. We'll make it."

"I know. That's not what's bothering me," she said. She put her head into the curve of his shoulder. "I feel so sorry for Claude."

While June snuggled into Red's arms, Liz raised a shaking hand to knock at the door. She was there because she had to be. She had to talk to Dina. She'd thought about it until she couldn't bear it any more. She'd had to come. Now she was here.

The door opened. Dina grinned. "Oh, hi. I never thought

232

it was you. I figured maybe Red had come back to bother me again."

Liz followed Dina inside, watched her close the door. Stood firmly near it, ready to flee if she had to. "Red?"

"He heard about me and Claude and came to talk me out of it." Dina laughed. "Fat chance."

Liz knew it was no good, knew it was useless. But she still had to try. "He meant well, didn't he?"

"You too?" Dina demanded.

Softly, Liz said, "You hardly know Claude."

"I know him well enough," Dina snapped.

"You don't even know yourself."

"What's it to you?" Dina demanded.

Liz shivered. Maggie. Maggie. She said, "You remind me so much . . . so much sometimes . . . I want only the best for you . . ."

"I've heard," Dina said. "Your sister. I know what you mean." Now Dina's voice was soft too. "It's funny. This feeling I get . . . It's why I asked if you'd be maid of honor—"

"If you went away for a little while even . . . Just waited to see. Perhaps then, you and Claude . . ."

Dina picked up the teddy bear, hugged it. Her eyes snapped sparks at Liz. "So you're against me too! You, along with the rest of them. Well, we'll show you! Claude and I. We will. We'll show you!"

Liz backed slowly from the room, closed the door behind her, wishing she hadn't come.

CHAPTER 19

The day before Claude had moved Dina out of the Hilton and settled her in the house. There was no reason to wait, and he didn't want to. Dina agreed it was a good idea.

Nothing happened to disturb them. Claude was more than ever convinced that once the town understood that he and Dina were to be together, no matter what, it would give up and leave him alone.

They had spent the night in each other's arms. Now she pressed against him. Her belly warm, silky. Her breasts round. Her slim thighs fitting his as if molded to their form.

"Tomorrow this time, when we wake up, you'll be my wife," he said.

Her voice was a husky, hesitant whisper. "It means so much to you, Claude."

He didn't know why, but he was afraid. She didn't sound like Maggie then. His arms tightened around her, tightened until she could hardly breathe, until she knew she was being crushed, absorbed. She struggled, cried, "Hey, stop! You're hurting me."

He eased his arms quickly, but didn't let her go. "I'm sorry. I didn't mean to. I was thinking of how it's what I always wanted. Always. You and me. And how it's going to be."

"I know." She smiled, stroked his face. "I do know. Believe me." But then she freed herself. "It's time, isn't it? Don't you think we should get started?"

He agreed that it must be without looking at his watch. He had been noticing the light in the room for a long while now. He hadn't wanted to leave her. Not even for the little while it would take him to get ready.

He said, "Stay in bed. I won't be slow. I'm too anxious." When she nodded, turned her head into the pillow, he went into the bathroom.

Shaving carefully, much more so than usual, he studied his face in the mirror. High cheekbones. Sunken eyes. A ruff of hair. He nicked his chin, and swore softly at the bright spot of blood that appeared.

Soon. Soon she'd be his wife. His Dina. His Maggie come back for him. His love.

He wondered if she knew. If she remembered another, younger Maggie. It didn't matter. She was his first and only love. How many men could have again what they'd already lost once?

Showered, he came out. She lay still, a small hump under the quilt, the teddy bear near her head. At first he thought she was asleep again. But then he saw that her eyes were wide open, gleaming with slivers of reflected light.

"Okay. Your turn," he said.

235

She didn't move. She didn't hear him. She saw his lips shape the words through a faint mist, a faint, flaky mist that had drifted through the silent room. There was something she had to remember but she couldn't figure out what it was.

He came and leaned over her and touched her forehead with his lips. A sudden anger swept her. Hot. Fierce. It freed her. She jerked away. His voice came through the mist. She saw his joyous face.

"Dina. Okay now."

"Yes." she smiled. "You go down and wait for me."

"I'd like to watch you dress." He had imagined it. Her arms behind her, hooking her skirt, thrusting her breasts forward. The smoothness of her throat.

"That's for tomorrow. And always. Today I want to be a surprise. I want to get ready and be beautiful for you."

He kissed her gently, then turned away. When he finished dressing, he went to the door. "I'll be waiting for you."

"It won't be too long," she promised.

She listened to his footsteps recede down the hallway, then from the stairs. Happy footsteps. Long, sloping strides that pulled his body on in graceless lurches. Sloping shoulders and big hands. The hot, fierce anger swept her again. Why? What about? It didn't make sense to her. To escape it, she scrambled from the bed. Instead of beginning preparations for her wedding day, she walked slowly around the room.

They'd be coming back here. In a few weeks, they'd begin the redecorating. It would be a beautiful room. She should be happy to think of it. But she wasn't.

She wished someone were with her. A girl should have someone. But it was Liz she was thinking about. It would be nice now to giggle with Liz. But Liz was against her. Dina had

236

known that since Liz had come and said maybe she should go away. Wait a little while. What was there to wait for? Claude had said only that Liz wouldn't be there with Richard. She couldn't make it. But Dina knew more, though she didn't say so, didn't even tell him about Liz's visit. Dina knew that Liz didn't like her. Liz was, plainly, in a way that didn't make sense, even a little scared of Dina. Dina knew it. She didn't know why.

Slowly, she went to the closet. Half of it was filled with what she had brought with her to Meadowville. Those plain skirts and blouses in drab colors that she disliked so much, but somehow couldn't bring herself to throw away or give away. She didn't know why. She did know that sometimes when she knew she wasn't going to be interrupted, she put them on and looked at herself in the mirror.

It was funny that she still didn't remember. Not where she'd been before she came here. Not who she'd been. Or what. Not where she had been going. Not what had happened as she walked across the parking lot near the Hilton. Everybody had said it would come back to her. She'd been certain it would. But it was still all blank, a shadow-filled emptiness that she was beginning now to believe would never be replaced with the sharp, clear images of memory.

It was funnier still that sometimes, when she least expected it, she was so struck with the sense of having passed that way before. People whose faces she'd almost recognized. People she knew she'd never known, and seemed to have seen somewhere. Places too. Main Street. The bus depot. Even Willie Harker's office, and the gas station next to it, except that she always had the feeling that Harker's pumps ought to be painted blue and white instead of yellow and red.

237

A car drove slowly along the road outside. She went to look, wondering who drove it and what he was doing on Vickery Street at that hour. It occurred to her that downstairs Claude might be watching it, too. Claude, scared that maybe on his wedding day somebody would pitch garbage into his front yard. She imagined spilling oranges peels, and coffee grounds, and soiled yellow napkins. Garbage instead of rice on her wedding day. She thought it but felt nothing. This was how Meadowville was. Against Claude. Poor Claude. She shrugged, turned away. And then, suddenly, the hot, fierce anger swept her again. Damn them! What were they trying to do? If they thought they'd drive Claude out, then they were crazy. She wouldn't let him. She'd make him stay until . . . until . . . She didn't know what for sure . . .

She began now to hurry. As she crossed to the bathroom she heard Claude walking in the downstairs hall. He'd left the window when the strange car had passed the house. He was on his way to the kitchen. She smiled. Maybe he'd have coffee ready for her.

She didn't hear the ringing of the phone as she splashed in the tub.

But Claude did. He stared at it, letting it go on until he'd counted ten. He was afraid to pick it up. Maybe there'd be no one there. Maybe this was a sign that the harassing was to begin again. Finally, when he couldn't stand it any more, he answered. It was his editor calling to say that the lost drawing had been delivered. Claude thanked him, hung up. He smiled grimly. Leaving the tracer with Bubba, the clerk at the post office, had apparently worked. Maybe it was a good sign.

An hour later, Dina started downstairs. She was powdered and perfumed. Her eyes were made up with blue shadow and liner, and sparkled from beneath long and darkened lashes. She wore a winter white dress, very tight in the bodice and full in the skirt. At the neck she wore a single strand of the pearls that Claude had given her. Over the outfit she had put on a winter white coat with a tiny collar of mink. Also a gift from Claude.

He stood waiting, watching.

Her face was aglow. Her small, slender body was enticing. She laughed. "You're staring at me, Claude."

He nodded, couldn't speak. The stammer was caught in his throat. Choking him. Strangling him. It was like before. As he remembered it. The two of them. Together. Just the two of them, setting out on a wonderful journey. And then . . . But this time it would be different. They would go to the county seat, and Richard would be with them.

First they would have a champagne lunch at the country club. It was all arranged. And Richard was bringing the flowers for Maggie. Richard. The flowers. The champagne lunch. They were different. But for the rest, it was the same. Maggie and he. Setting out alone. To be married.

"This is the happiest day of my life. Because of you." And he wondered why the words sounded so familiar. Had he said them before? He went on, eager, joyful, "And I'm going to make you happy, and take care of you forever."

She sank down to the bottom step. Her slim fingers slowly stroked the mink at her collar. Her shining eyes stared into his face. She gave a long, discontented sigh. "I wish you wouldn't talk like that."

"Dina! What?" His head spun around to face her. "What?" he said again.

"Talk like that. You know. About forever. About the future."

There was a flaky mist rising between them. It was as if they hung in space. Just the two of them. And beyond there was nothingness. She didn't remember now that when she started down the steps, she had been thinking, *Soon. Soon,* and that she had known then what the word meant. Everything, these last months, had been directed to the coming moment that she thought of as *soon.* Her laugh, her dancing walk. Her fingers lingering on his cheek. All that had disappeared into the flaking white mist.

And he, face gray now, cried, "But why? Why shouldn't I talk of the future? We're getting married today. We're going down to the county seat with Richard, and . . ."

"No," she told him, shaking her flaming head. "No. No. We can't. We mustn't"

His eyes sank deep into his head. He whispered hoarsely, "What're you talking about?"

She moaned softly. She felt as if she were being torn to pieces from inside. Pushed one way. Pulled another. An ice storm whirled within her head. She clutched her head with both hands, gasping.

"What's the matter?" he yelled desperately.

"I wanted to," she said. "I did. I did, Claude. It was what I wanted all along. To marry you. To be with you. I did. I must have. Of course that's what I wanted." But the more she said it, the more unsure she was. She had wanted him. But for what? "And then, when I came down, I saw . . ." What had she seen? She didn't know. She just knew she mustn't marry Claude. She said softly, "I was going to try to tell you gently. Kindly. I started wrong. I'm sorry. I don't want to hurt you. But I can't do it." Her gleaming eyes were suddenly sad, filled with tears. "Believe me, I'm so sorry. But somehow, I know it's wrong. I have to . . . I have to know who I am. We can't pretend it didn't happen. My memory, I mean. I can't forget it. So until I know . . . until I find out who I am . . ."

"We know who you are," he said. "You're Maggie."

She stared at him for a long, blank moment. As the white mist faded his anguished face became clear. Then, rising, she laughed loudly. A bitter and ugly sound. A mirthless taunt. It twisted her face and brought flames flickering into her eyes. "Marry you?" she screamed, the hot, fierce anger engulfing her. "Marry *you!* What for? Why should I? Who are you? A Vickery, so what? You're nothing but the town clown. That's who. Nobody likes you or wants you. You haven't a friend in the world. And me, me, I'm somebody. I can do anything I want." She did a small pirouette, toes pointed and arms lifted. "I can go to Hollywood and be a star. I can marry a rich man. Why would I go with you to nothing? When I can have everything."

He backed away from her, hearing distant sounds echoing down the long corridor of years. He whispered, "Maggie! Maggie!"

"You see," she said, her voice suddenly soft, and with no cruel laughter in it. "You see? You don't even know who I am."

"But you love me," he pleaded. "You told me. We made our plans. We can't go back now."

"I wondered how far you'd go. And now I've found out."

She was laughing again, a shrill sound that hurt her ears. "You'll go as far as I let you. Well, I won't let you. What right do you have to my life?"

"Maggie!" he screamed.

"Damn you," she cried. "Damn you forever."

He couldn't stand her strident voice. He couldn't stand what she was saying. He knew there was more, but he turned and fled. Outside, weeping, he threw himself into the Volare and drove away as fast as he could.

Dina came slowly out of the house. Clutching the rail she let herself down the stairs. She looked after him. Even as she saw the car disappear down the street she reached out, as if to hold him. "Wait, Claude," she cried. "Wait. That's not how I meant to tell you. In a little while, something will happen. I'll remember . . . I'll remember . . ."

But he was gone. And so was the street, the light. She stared into a thickening white mist, while an ice storm whirled in her head. With numbing lips she whispered, "Claude, wait!."

Then she fell. . . .

There were other words in Claude's ear. Words rushing at him from the bitter wind that blew on his wet face. A horn blared at him. A car pulled up behind him, raced frantically to keep up for a few moments. He quickly left it behind. He wasn't even aware of it, the noise of the horn, Richard's shout. He didn't see the snowy fields, the blue sky, the sunlight for today, his wedding day.

He heard nothing but the voices in his head. He saw nothing but the flash of headlights cutting through the shadows of Dead Man's Bluff, a faint dusting of lights in the valley below and the bright spire of the distant church.

And Maggie was saying to him, "Turn back, Claude. I want to go home."

In that instant, dream turned into nightmare. . . .

It began at his father's funeral. He'd known what was coming. He could see the cupped hands over whispering mouths. The straight faces in which the eyes laughed with malicious triumph. Dane Vickery was a thief. A suicide. His father was dead. Dead. His father, whom he had always hated, loved. His father gone. The money was nothing. How could it have been? Dane was a rich man. If he took the money it was only to run away from memory. Nobody understood. Nobody but Claude. It was him. His own fault. Because he was born. His father had come to the end of bearing the awful loneliness which Claude himself knew. He had come to the end of it and refused it. Claude's birth had cost him love. And his father had died for it. So it was Claude's fault. And now he was alone. Except for Maggie.

But he already knew what would happen. He could tell from their faces. The Paiges. The Harkers. The Meeses. They'd turned against his father. And now they would turn against Claude. And he'd lose his Maggie. He had to have her. Had to. He couldn't live without her.

Behind shaking fingers, he whispered, with somber music as background, "Meet me, Maggie. The usual place."

She nodded and that was all. He went through the rest of it, waited for dark. And she was there, as she'd said she'd be. He was ready. Money in his wallet. Hope in his heart. Everything else left behind.

They drove for a while, then parked partway up Dead Man's

243

Bluff. They made love there in the dark. Her belly silky and warm against his. Her breasts filling his hands. Her tongue in his mouth.

Later he said, "If we go back, they'll end it for us."

"Let them try," she laughed. "I do what I want to do."

"Your father though. Your mother. You'll see. We don't have a chance against them."

"I'm not worried. And you shouldn't be. I can always get out. Nobody can stop me from what I want to do."

He held her tightly. "Listen, Maggie. I've got four hundred dollars with me. We could run away. Just the two of us. We'd go to St. Louis. I'd get a job. We'd always be together."

She looked into his eyes for a moment. Then her lips curled into a smile and she snuggled closer to him. "Okay, Claude. Let's do it."

In moments they were speeding up the hump of Dead Man's Bluff, and he was telling her how they'd get married and how he would make her happy forever.

He heard her giggle as she pulled away. "Oh, come on, Claude," she said, "you must be crazy. Why would I run away with you? What for?"

"To be with me. So they can't separate us. That's why we're doing it."

"No, Claude. No. I only said that to see how far you'd go. I want you to take me home."

Her hair was a glistening cloud around her face. Her eyes sparkled. He thought she was the most beautiful thing he had ever seen in his life, and she *was* his life. But she said, "Stop the car. I want you to turn around now. I want to go home."

He pulled over, weeping, choking. "If you run away with me, we can be together."

"But who wants to? Me? You think I want to be with you forever? Why should I? What can you do for me?"

"You have to. You told me . . ."

"I want to go home, Claude," she cried.

He grabbed her, hugging her tight. He wouldn't let her go. He wouldn't . . .

And now, fleeing through December sunlight, he remembered for the first time in ten years how his fingers had closed around her throat, while she screamed, "Let me go! You're hurting me. I hate you, Claude." His fingers in her throat while she fought him, crushed to him, with her arms around his neck. Even then, as she struggled, her arms were around his neck.

Suddenly she was still, limp. No breath on her lips. No light in her eyes.

Sobbing, he let her go, saw her fall to the seat. He started the car, went plunging upward into the shadows of Dead Man's Bluff and the headlights bounced off the black walls and the wheels jolted. The earth fell away and he and his Maggie spun into the dark.

When he staggered to his feet the car was ablaze. He reached through flame to pull her out. And her fiery arms held him until he fought free. . . .

He hadn't remembered how he'd killed his Maggie until Dina said she wouldn't have him. Dina. Maggie. What he believed the truth was after he'd slowly rebuilt himself was what he'd wished it had been. Dina. Maggie.

It was Maggie who had brought him back to Meadowville. Maggie, calling to him. He'd had a ten-year appointment with Maggie. Now he knew why. It was so he would remember.

But he couldn't bear it. Screaming, weeping, he drove wildly along the hump of Dead Man's Bluff, wheels screeching as the

Volare careened from curve to curve. Until, at the top, where it had happened to him ten years before, the car lurched and jolted and the rear end swung out, and the wheels bit into crumbling earth and asphalt. There was a shaking as the world turned upside down. A shaking and thunder and the blackness of an unending night.

Then he was flying. And then there was nothing.

Richard, half a mile away, heard the blast. He rounded a curve and saw flames leap for the sky.

He stopped in mid-road, knowing what he would see. A pyre as bright as December sunlight rose from the foot of the bluff. The Volari, engulfed in fire, lay on its side. There was no sign of Claude.

Richard flung himself down the slope. His dark suit was ripped by the underbrush. His shoes split. His hands bled at the palms from bramble scratches. But he didn't notice. Swearing softly, shocked beyond thought, he stumbled as close to the burning car as he dared. Thick, black, oily smoke drove him back. He yelled Claude's name. There was no response. Nothing but the leap of flame in endless silence. Shoulders slumping, he climbed to the road. . . .

Chapter 20

Liz heard the sirens, but she was in a hurry and didn't pay any attention to them.

Richard had said they'd leave the Vickery house at eleven. He'd told her everything about the arrangements. Although she hadn't listened, hadn't wanted to know, she remembered.

She had been up most of the night. She had dark circles under her eyes, which she powdered away quickly, her hands trembling. She'd torn her panty hose in putting them on and had had to change.

All through the sleepless night, remembering how Richard had looked when he left her, she had tried to decide what to do. Stubborn. Loyal. Ready to fight if he had to. That was Richard.

But she couldn't fight. Finally she'd begun to pack. St. Louis. A new life. It was the only way. Leave everything behind. Run.

In a little while she'd be gone for good. Someday she would forget. Again she told herself it was the only way. To save herself. Her sanity. To stop thinking what she kept thinking.

She pulled on her heavy storm boots, got into her coat. It took only a short time to load the car. Before she locked up, she took a tour of the house.

Her mother's room. She looked at the silver bell, but didn't touch it. *You pay for my sins,* her mother had said. What sins? Liz shook her head, backed slowly from the room. The snapshot of her parents in the living room. She studied it for a long moment before turning away. Her mother. Her father. They were like strangers now. Her own room. Childhood dreams and expectations. Long nights wishing for Richard to lie beside her, hold her in his arms. She hurried out. Then, last, the one that had been Maggie's. It had been empty for a long time, but her presence was still there. Maggie, by turns sweet and then suddenly bitter. Extravagant, careless, determined to have her own way. Then so joyfully loving. Liz, knowing, seeing, foreswearing judgment, had loved her, and loved her still. Loving never stopped, she told herself, and gently closed the door behind her.

Everything was in order. One day she'd return for a little while, empty the house, sell it. Then it would be over.

As she started the car she heard sirens. She wondered briefly what was happening, then told herself she didn't care. Meadowville was no longer her concern.

At Main Street, stopped for a traffic light, she glanced at her watch. It was ten forty-five. Richard would be at Claude's by now.

He had said he would be. So she could depend on it. He'd be doing what he felt was right, necessary, as he always had. If he'd been different, she wouldn't have loved him, and he wouldn't have been Richard. And she'd blamed him for it, allowing his loyalty to Claude to become disloyalty to her.

She knew that she couldn't leave without seeing him. He needed her. And she had to be with him. Just one more time. To stand beside him when Claude and Dina were married.

Her heart jumped. The light changed. She didn't notice. She had to do it for Richard. Not for Claude and Dina. She wouldn't even look at them.

But for Richard. So he wouldn't feel alone. The town was against him. He'd said Claude and Dina had to have someone. But he had to have someone, too. And who should it be but Liz? Liz, whom he loved, who loved him.

One last time with him. And afterward she would leave for St. Louis.

The light turned green. Breathless, frightened, she turned the car around. The streets were empty, still. Snow banks lined them, and overhead the trees glittered in silvery sheaths of ice. She tried not to think. Except that she was going to Richard. To be with him. So it would be the two of them.

But she was still scared. She knew she would be until she left Meadowville behind. A chill clung to her under her heavy coat. Her teeth were chattering by the time she approached the Vickery house. From the corner she could see that Claude's Volari was gone. And that Richard's car wasn't there, either.

She pulled in, braked, jumped out. If she could get into the house, she'd phone the country club. Richard would come and pick her up. There was still time. She could be with him.

The gate swung wide. The snow crunched underfoot as she turned in and hurried up the path.

Midway she stopped.

Dina lay sprawled at the foot of the steps. Her white coat was spread around her. A white cheek, made paler by contrast to flaming hair, pressed into light mink. Her sightless eyes stared at the cold blue sky. Her breathless mouth hung open. She was dead.

No dancing walk . . . no laughter . . . nothing of Maggie lay here.

Sobbing, Liz rushed up the stairs and through the half-open door into the house. Inside she managed to stammer a few words into the phone before it fell from her numbed fingers.

Weeping still, she went outside again.

No dancing walk . . . no laughter . . . nothing of Maggie here . . .

Lines fanning from the corners of blue eyes . . . thin rim of blond gleaming at the roots of dyed flaming red hair . . .

Liz heard her mother's voice . . . *I know you think I'm crazy. But I can't help it. I know that Maggie will come back. . . .*

Claude had had nothing to do with it. It had begun long before he had returned. Her mother had been a sick, grief-destroyed woman. Why had Liz listened to her? Why had she allowed herself to become afraid? She didn't know. And it didn't matter any more. She was free now. It was over.

She pulled off her coat, knelt. A bad dream, but fading. A familiarity gone forever.

As a shadow fell on her, she looked up. A cloud drifting across the sun. As she watched the cloud moved on and the shadow was gone. It had been like that up to now. A cloud drifting before the sun.

She gently stroked Dina's cheek, then slipped off her own heavy coat and covered the girl. Dina . . . so alone, so frightened by not remembering, seizing upon the present because she had no past to cling to. And now it no longer mattered.

Liz remained on her knees, holding Dina's limp, cold hand . . .

That was how Richard found her when he hurried back from Claude's funeral pyre to tell Dina what had happened.

Liz saw him leap from the car, rush toward her. He was gray, his face set in stone. She knew instantly there was more to come. As he slipped and crunched his way through the snow, she knew that she couldn't leave him. Her thoughts were mere fragments. Swift recognitions. *You pay for my sins,* her mother had said. Speaking of guilt. Her own. Liz faced what she had nearly done to herself, to Richard . . . guilt . . . because she'd resented the burdens she carried, and then her mother had died . . . Unable to accept it, she'd blamed Claude, thus Richard . . . The breach to separate them because she felt undeserving of love when her own love proved wanting . . . But Liz had loved her mother . . . tried . . . failed only to protect her against inevitable death.

Richard looked down at Dina, touched Liz's shoulder.

She stumbled to her feet, her blue eyes hot, blazing, fixed on his face. "I have to tell you. It was all true. What you said. About the town. About everything. And Dina and Claude, too." And, in a steady whisper, "Can we get married right away?"

She didn't have to explain, say any more. He understood. He glanced once more at Dina, then he opened his coat, drew Liz inside and buttoned it around her. He held her tightly, his body warming hers, while he told her about Claude's death on Dead Man's Bluff.

Together, holding each other, they stood beside Dina, waiting until help came.

EPILOGUE

Five days later Claude and Dina were buried side by side in the same cemetery as the rest of the Vickerys, not far from where the Paiges lay.

By then it was believed that Dina Forrest had died of a brain embolism. It was considered probably a long-delayed effect caused by a blow on the head suffered during the attack in which she had lost her memory. Everyone thought that Claude had found her body and, always unbalanced, had driven wildly away to commit suicide on Dead Man's Bluff.

The whole of Meadowville was present at the brief services.

On New Year's Day the whole of Meadowville gathered once again, and when Richard and Liz left the minister's study in which they had just been married, they were showered with rice and roses, and ran, laughing, through the drifting snow to set out on their St. Louis honeymoon.

When they returned home, he began the process that would end with the town gaining all of the Vickery property.

Eventually, but for a few years only, there would be a recreation center where Dane and John and Claude had once lived. Then a new building would be put up, and the old Vickery house would become known as Stanton Place, where Red and June would prosper, and raise three sets of twins.

Vernon Meese would be elected mayor after the Council of Aldermen was abolished. He would serve ten years, and then become governor of the state.

Willie Harker would sell his gas station and used-car business, and he and his wife would retire to a pleasant life in Arizona.

By then both men would be millionaires.

Computo-Sales would have built a giant industrial complex on the outskirts of town, and traffic would be heavy seven nights a week on Main Street. There would be a new airport twenty-five miles away.

Richard's practice would grow. A time would come when he would sit on the bench of the circuit court that had once been Morgan Paige's.

He and Liz would have three sons, each so like Richard that Liz would look at them and smile, thinking that they were all Braun and that there were no Paiges left in Meadowville any more. In marriage Liz and Richard would be even closer than most wives and husbands, but there was one thing he would never share with her. In the first year of their marriage, he would try to find out about the girl who had lost her memory, to learn who she had been and where she was going when she came to Meadowville. He had her identification, found in her purse when she was brought to the hospital by Red Stanton. Richard had turned the case over to the best investigative agency in New York. It came up with nothing. Nobody knew her at her given address. Nobody had ever heard of her. After a while Richard would give up. But he would never stop wondering about her. And he would never tell Liz that every lead proved to be a dead end, and that he had never found a trace of Dina Forrest or anyone who had ever known her.

All Futura Books are available at your bookshop or newsagent, or can be ordered from the following address:
Futura Books, Cash Sales Department,
P.O. Box 11, Falmouth, Cornwall.

Please send cheque or postal order (no currency), and allow 45p for postage and packing for the first book plus 20p for the second book and 14p for each additional book ordered up to a maximum charge of £1.63 in U.K.

Customers in Eire and B.F.P.O. please allow 45p for the first book, 20p for the second book plus 14p per copy for the next 7 books, thereafter 8p per book.

Overseas customers please allow 75p for postage and packing for the first book and 21p per copy for each additional book.